Say You Love Me

There are some guys you just can't forget.

There are some guys that catch your eye.

There are some guys you just can't say no to.

Cody Brookstone. He's my best friend's brother. I've known him for years. Fancied him for what seems like forever. And of course, he's never noticed me. I've always been his sister Mila's annoying friend, but I'm about to change that. Mila came up with a plan for me to snag him. I'm going to make him mine. One way or another. The plan is fail proof. Well, not really. There are plenty of things that can go wrong. Plenty of ways that my heart could get broken. But what's the path to true love without some risk?

There are some girls you can't get out of your mind.

There are some girls that can break your heart.

There are some girls that make you rethink everything.

Sally Johnson. My sister's best friend. Sweet, funny, always there. She's got one of those smiles that makes you happy and a body that goes on for days, if you know what I mean. She's crept into my life, making me feel things I don't understand. I can't give her what she wants. Even if I love giving her what she needs. Or rather what I need. I didn't expect everything to go crazy. I didn't expect for everything to get out of hand. Now I've gone and got myself in a mess that I don't understand and can't fix easily. Sally's the one girl that's got me thinking that maybe, just maybe, I don't know it all.

Say You Love Me

J. S. Cooper

Thank you for purchasing Say You Love Me.
To be notified of all my new releases, please join my
MAILING LIST!
http://eepurl.com/bpCvd1

Editing by Lorelei Logsdon

Contents

Acknowledgments and Dedications

Sometimes we fall in love with someone because we have an immediate connection with them. Sometimes people come into our lives and we just know that they are someone important. They will make an impact. They will flip our hearts upside down and inside out. And our lives will never be the same. Sometimes this love works out and we end up with the loves of our lives. And sometimes, sometimes, the fairytale is not meant to be. However, there is something special in that love, something special in that moment of time. And sometimes we just need to figure out what that love means to us.

This book is dedicated to every single one of us that has fallen in love with someone and gone through the pain of not knowing if we were good enough. Always remember that you are always good enough. And the right guy will know. And when he knows and you know, that's when you both know. That's when it's true love!

There are so many people I need to thank for making this book happen. First and foremost, all of my readers that requested a story for Sally and Cody. They were bit characters in the Four Week Fiancé series, but they really resonated with a lot of people. Thank you to all the readers that have purchased, reviewed, talked about, and loved my books. Your support means everything to me and it is for you that I write. I would like to thank the J. S. Cooper Street Team, made up of readers and friends who provide me daily support and encouragement. I appreciate your kind words and love more than you'll ever know. I also need to thank my assistant Katrina Jaekley for typing up handwritten pages and always pushing me forward to continue writing. I'd like to thank all of my beta readers: Stacy Hahn, Tanya Kay Skaggs, Kathy Shreve, Cilicia White, Nancy Murtha, Tammie Lynd, Sarah Ackerman, Laura McMillin, Gwen Midgyett, Kristine Roller, Kyna Mack, Julianna Santiago, Heather Coombes, LAci Keenzel, Jennifer Pon, and Kim Briesemeister. Your feedback as I wrote the book encouraged me to keep going with the words in my head.

As always, I thank God for all of my blessings and for the ability to write for a living.

I hope everyone enjoys this book as much as I enjoyed writing it.

Jaimie
XOXO

PROLOGUE

Sally

CODY BROOKSTONE. MY first love. He's my best friend's brother. The man of my dreams. He's everything I've ever wanted and yet, he barely knows I exist as more than a friend. He is the most handsome man I've ever seen in my life: six feet, two inches of muscular brawn, dark blond hair, hazel eyes that go from green to brown on a whim, and a smile that lights up my heart. His very presence does things to me that I can't explain. Cody Brookstone is the man I've had a crush on for what seems like forever. There are so many declarations I want to make to him. Declarations that make my heart flutter. Declarations like:

"I will wait for you because I don't want anyone else."

"I will wait for you because I'm a fool."

"I will wait for you because the feeling in my heart is greater than anything I've ever felt before in my life."

"I will wait for you because the smile on your face makes me happy when I'm sad."

"I will wait for you because I love you."

I wanted to tell him all of those things. I wanted him to know how much I loved him. I wanted him to know I would wait a lifetime for him. I would have told him all of those things, too, if I thought it would mean anything. All I needed was for him to say he loved me. Three simple words. That's all I needed. "I love you." That's all I needed to hear. At least that's what I thought in the beginning.

Have you ever been in love? Have you ever been in love so bad that it hurts you in places that you didn't even know existed inside of you? Have you ever thought of someone so much that you thought you could read their mind? That somehow they were a part of you, that indelibly you were linked by something greater than words or feelings or actions? That your connection was created by God himself? Have you ever had that feeling? That feeling where you feel so high, so happy, so powerful, just being around them? Their smile makes you smile. Their laugh lights up your life, so that nothing could dim it. Absolutely nothing. Just being there with them, just talking to them, touching them, seeing them, knowing them gives you something that you can't explain. That's power. Real power. And that power is dangerous. It's dangerous because you lose yourself to that feeling. And sometimes when you lose yourself in that way to the wrong person...well, sometimes, you never get yourself back.

I've experienced that love. Great love. Love so powerful that I couldn't eat or sleep for days. Only, he didn't love me. He didn't want me. He didn't feel the same way. And the pain that I felt, the pain I carried inside of me, well it nearly broke me. You see, it didn't make sense to me. How can one love someone so greatly and they don't feel a thing? It doesn't make sense. It didn't make sense. I thought that was the worst of it. I thought that was the end of the world, but I was wrong. I thought Cody Brookstone breaking my heart was the end of it all, but really it was only the beginning.

You see, I've gone and found myself in an even more precarious situation. A situation that has called everything I thought I knew into question. A situation that has made me doubt every feeling and every emotion I ever had. A situation that makes me wonder what true love really is. Everything I believed in has come crashing down around me.

Now I don't know if him telling me he loves me will mean anything.

Now I don't know if my world will ever be the same again.

Now I don't know what I feel for Cody Brookstone, and I don't know if I can find it in my heart to figure out the answers to any of my questions before it's too late.

PART I

CHAPTER ONE

Sally

WHEN I WAS just a little girl, I always read fairytales, and I loved hearing how the handsome prince would fall in love with the princess and sweep her away. He'd love her with everything in him and he'd do everything he could to protect her. I always thought I'd find that love. It's all I've ever really craved. There was something so comforting knowing that there was someone in the world who loved you more than life itself. My childhood was pretty normal I suppose. My parents divorced when I was barely three and I was shuttled back and forth between them for the next eight years of my life. Then my dad moved back to Guyana, in South America, to take over his family business and all of a sudden I went to seeing him once every couple of years and talking to him on the phone every few months. My dad remarried, though he had no more kids, and I felt like his new relationship took precedence over his role in my life. His new wife hated me because she was a jealous cow and I was a reminder of his loving another woman. My mom, well, she sort of drifted about life aimlessly after the divorce, never knowing if she was coming or going and the bitterness of her marriage ending never seemed to leave her. I'm lucky I didn't become bitter and jaded myself, but I think that was thanks to having Mila as a best friend and having her family as a surrogate.

It didn't hurt that I found Cody mesmerizing and that he was on my mind all the time. I suppose my unhealthy obsession began the first time I met him. Even though we were young, it was love at first sight for me. He was the golden boy, all dimples and big smiles, teasing and loving and full of life. When I was around Cody, I forgot about everything else. I forgot about being scared of exams, the loneliness of going home, the heartache of rejection when a boy I had a crush on didn't like me. I forgot about being hungry, angry, sad, mad—whatever emotions I was experiencing at the time. It was like time stood still when I was with him. We were just us, at a moment in time, and nothing else mattered. I can remember the exact moment when I knew he was my true love. I can remember it as if it happened yesterday. We were at the lake house and we'd gone for a walk. It was just been the two of us and I was so happy to have some alone time with him. We stared out at the lake, under the moonlight, and we just gazed at the rippling water in amazement.

"It's so beautiful," I said softly. "How amazing would it feel to fall asleep in the water and let it carry you away gently?"

"Pretty amazing, I suppose," Cody said quietly, nodding as we stood there.

"The only issue I see," I continued, "is if you floated off into the middle of the lake, though I suppose that would be scarier if it were an ocean. Then you'd float off into the middle of nowhere."

"That would be pretty scary." He nodded. "Though I suppose we could be like the otters."

"Be like the otters?" I asked curiously, turning to look at him. "What do you mean?"

"You don't know about the otters?" He turned to look down at me and his eyes were sparkling in delight as he stared at me.

7

"No, tell me," I said, gazing back at him, wanting his eyes to never leave mine.

"When otters fall asleep in the water, they make sure to hold hands so that they don't drift apart. So even if the water carries them downstream, they're still together."

"Oh wow," I said simply, my heart melting at how sweet that sounded.

"So we could be like them," he said with a small smile. "We can go and fall asleep in the lake and let the water take us where it may, but we'll have to hold hands to make sure that we don't drift apart."

"That sounds like a good idea to me." I grinned up at him, my heart overflowing with love. "That sounds like a really good idea."

YOU EVER HAVE that moment where you see a guy and your whole body freezes still and then turns hot? Your heart starts beating fast and your stomach flips over and over and over and all you can think is *Oh hot damn, that man is smoking hot and I want him right now. I want him to look at me, smile at me, run up to me, grab me, pull me into his arms, kiss me hard, and then run his finger down my cheek and tell me I'm the woman he's been waiting for his whole life.* You ever experience that? Some people call it love at first sight. Others call it lust at first sight. Still others call it a chemical imbalance. I call it what I feel for Cody Brookstone every time I see him. He's that one guy I can't get out of my blood. That guy I've fancied for more years than I like to think of. His is the smile I see when I think of dying or getting married. Either one. Not that I think of dying often. Or getting married. Though sometimes I can be slightly morbid. Sometimes I think to myself, would Cody care if I died? Would he love me then? Would he want me then? Yeah, I'm a sad case. I think about Cody every single day, without fail. Even when I'm trying not to think about him. Some people would call me obsessed. They'd say I'm like the girl from *Fatal Attraction*. Only, perhaps I'm worse. I've never dated Cody. I've never kissed him. Never slept with him. Never even held hands with him. Cody Brookstone doesn't even know I exist. Well, as a woman. He knows I exist as a human being. I'm best friends with his sister, Mila. And no, that hasn't gotten me any brownie points. If anything, it's made me even more hands-off. To be fair, I don't know if Cody would have wanted me even if I weren't friends with Mila. He's the kind of guy who likes to have fun. I can't think of any girl he's dated seriously or for a super long time. Which used to make me happy. But now it makes me wonder why. It's not like his parents had this crazy shady marriage or that's he's been super terribly hurt by an ex. From what I know, he's never had his heart broken. Or even been in love. Which makes me both happy and sad. I'm a terrible romantic, so it makes me think *Ooh well maybe I'm his true love, his one and only.* It makes my heart beat rapidly when I think of him telling me he loves me. Oh my God, could you even imagine how that would feel? Having him tell me he loves me, that I'm the only woman he's ever loved? It would be like something out of a movie. Something that we'd tell our kids and grandkids. Something I would dream about in my grave (I told you I was morbid). I know, I know. I'm unrealistic and a dreamer. And probably too old for these sorts of pipe dreams.

I don't know how some women seem to have it so easy. They blink and they get the guy they want. I blink and I smudge my mascara and eyeliner and end up looking like a skunk or raccoon. Never mind getting the guy to notice me. Unless of course he notices the eyes and wonders if I'm okay because I look like I've been crying or beaten. That's my luck.

Not that it mattered. Because there I was, standing on Cody's doorstep, waiting for him to answer the door and let me into his apartment. This was going to be my moment. I was going to make my move. To make Cody Brookstone fall in love with me. Or at least take me to his bed. I deserved that at least, right? Hot sex is better than nothing. At least that's what I kept telling myself.

I took a deep breath before I knocked on the front door. My heart was in my mouth. I, for some reason only known to God, was hoping that today was going to be the day that my luck changed and Cody suddenly looked at me and told me he loved me. I knew it wasn't realistic. I knew life didn't go like that. And I knew I was only looking for more heartache. He wasn't going to just fall in love with me like that. This wasn't the movies. I'd known him for so long and he'd never fallen for me. Not even when I looked super hot in short skirts and tight dresses. Not even the time I 'accidentally' walked into his bedroom in only my underwear. Not even the time we'd gone to the hot tub and I'd worn my tightest, skimpiest bikini. I hadn't even seen him giving me a look of appreciation. It was sad. I was a sad case. I wasn't sure how I'd let it get to this point. I felt like I was wasting my life away waiting for him to fall in love with me. But I just couldn't stop. I was hoping for the fairytale, but I wasn't sure the fairytale would ever happen for me. Ever.

Cody opened the front door before I had a chance to knock or ring the doorbell. "Hey stranger, why're you just standing on the doorstep?"

"Sorry, I was daydreaming." I smiled at him, giving him my most winning smile, trying to position my face in an angle that showed off my features the best.

"Come on in. Mila and TJ will be here in a second." He

stepped back and ushered me in. "TJ says the reservation for the go-karts is a little later than he'd originally thought, so we're going to grab dinner first."

"Awesome," I said as I stepped inside, slightly disappointed. He'd barely glanced at me, and certainly hadn't seemed to notice my new tight jeans or the cute top I'd bought especially for the occasion. I followed him down the corridor to his living room and tried to stifle my sigh. I was an idiot for feeling upset. I wasn't sure what I'd been expecting, but I had hoped for more than I'd gotten. But maybe it wouldn't be so bad. I mean, we were still spending the evening together.

"So I'm just going to go and finish up an email." He gave me a grin as he stood in the doorway of the living room and ushered me in. "Have a seat and I'll be right back."

"Oh, okay." I nodded and walked over to his couch and sat down. I looked at him for a few seconds and then back at my lap.

"Here's the remote. You can watch some TV if you want." He handed it to me and our fingers brushed for a few seconds and I felt a secret thrill running through me. I looked up at him to see if he'd felt it too, but he didn't even look at me.

"Oh yeah, you want something to drink?" He stopped and looked back at me, his eyes friendly, if nothing else, as he glanced at me. "Sorry, I'm a bad host sometimes."

"I'm okay, thanks," I said as I shook my head. "Plus I know where the kitchen is, so I can help myself if I get thirsty."

"Yeah, you can." He laughed and nodded. "Just don't go snooping."

"What would I go snooping for?" I questioned him, slightly annoyed.

"Who knows why you and Mila like to snoop?"

"What are you afraid I'll find?"

"Ha, you don't want to know." He wiggled his eyebrows at me.

"I do want to know. That's why I'm asking."

"Big man stuff." He winked at me.

"As opposed to little man stuff?" I tilted my head to the side.

"As opposed to little boy stuff." He laughed. "I don't know what a little man is." He paused. "Well, I know what a little man could be, and I'm certainly not a little man."

"Okay," I said, my face turning red at his words. I was pretty sure I knew what he was alluding to and I couldn't believe he'd said that to me.

"Sorry, that was inappropriate." He laughed. "But yeah, help yourself to whatever you want."

"I will." I nodded. "Does that include all the naughty stuff I find as well?"

"I can hook you up with some condoms if you think you'll be in need." He stared at me then, his eyes curious as he gazed at me.

"I'm fine, thanks."

"Good." He nodded, more seriously this time, the smile on his face not as huge. "How is your dating life going, anyway?"

"Great," I lied. "Almost too many men to keep up with."

"So, no one special?" He glanced at me for a second and then looked over my body before looking back at my face.

"Nope." I shook my head. *Only you, in my dreams.*

"Pity." He grinned.

"What about you?" I asked, even though my stomach was in knots waiting for his answer.

"Dating is fine. No one special, but then I'm not looking for anyone special." He laughed. "So I'm pretty cool with that."

"Yeah." I smiled at him, not sure if I was happy or sad at his words. Of course I was happy that he didn't have anyone special, but I was also sad that he didn't want anyone special. And I wanted to know what he meant by 'dating was fine'. How many women was he dating? And who were they and what did they look like and how often was he dating them and how much did he like them and oh... I had so many questions, so many things I wanted to know, but didn't really want to know. I was going to drive myself crazy just thinking about it.

"Sally?" He touched my shoulder and I looked up at him in surprise.

"Yeah?" I asked him, frowning.

"You seemed to space out. You okay?" He walked over and sat down on the couch.

"I'm fine." I nodded. "I thought you needed to work."

"It can wait." He leaned back on the couch. "How are you feeling?"

"About what?" I gulped. Oh, my God, did he know I was in love with him?

"Mila and TJ," he continued. "I'm sure you must be feeling sad now that Mila is spending so much time with TJ. I know you guys used to spend a lot of time together. I mean, I know I barely see TJ now and we used to spend a lot of time together. So I can only imagine what it's like for you and Mila, because you guys were joined at the hip."

"Oh, okay, yeah, it's been hard—different." I gave him a weak smile. "I mean, I'm so happy for them. I know Mila has wanted to be with TJ for a long time, but now it's almost like she's replaced my friendship."

"She could never replace your friendship," Cody said. "You know that, right?"

"Well, yeah, but you know what I mean. TJ is the first person she goes to now. A lot of our friendship was spent talking about TJ and how much she loved him." I laughed. "And her being angsty about the relationship, but that's changed now. She has no need to be angsty about it. She has him and they're happy and well, it's just different."

"Is that why you've been so spacy?" He looked at me in concern. "You really shouldn't let it bother you so much."

"That's not why I've been spacy," I said, then stopped. "Well, kinda," I lied. Better for him to think I was worried about my friendship with Mila than for him to know I was obsessed with thinking about him. I definitely didn't want him to know how much time he spent in my head and dreams. I knew it was almost obsessive and would most likely make him think I was a nutcase. I mean, who stays in love with a man who barely knows she exists? I was an idiot, and the more I thought about the actual situation, the more I knew that it wasn't a healthy one to be in. I just didn't know how to get out of it.

"Well, you know that I…" Cody's voice trailed off and he jumped up as the doorbell rang. "Hmm, saved by the bell. That must be them."

"Yeah." I nodded, though I was curious as to what he'd been about to say.

"We can continue this talk later though, if you want to." He looked down at me and gave me such a warm look that my heart melted into pieces.

"Sure," I said and smiled up at him. How could I not love this man? He was so concerned for my feelings, even though he didn't love me. God, I wasn't sure how I was ever going to get over him.

"SALLY, YOU LOOK gorgeous." Mila hurried into the room and gave me a big hug, her long blond hair cascading down her shoulders, her cheeks bright and her eyes cheery.

"So do you." I gave her a huge hug and stared at her. "Being in love agrees with you."

"Haha, thanks." She grinned and looked back at TJ for a few seconds. I watched them exchanging a loving look and I turned away slightly, feeling envious. How horrible was it that I was jealous of my best friend? I was happy that she'd found love, but I was sad for myself. Would I ever find that? Would Cody ever look at me the way TJ looked at Mila?

"So what have you guys been up to?" Mila asked as she looked around the room. "Sorry we're late. Bad traffic."

"No worries." I shook my head. "We were just sitting on the couch, talking."

"Oh?" Her eyes brightened and I shook my head slightly, to indicate to her that it wasn't anything good or exciting.

"Just about random stuff." I gave her a quick smile and then leaned in to whisper in her ear, "I think I just need to forget Cody. I don't think it's ever going to happen."

"Oh Sally." She chewed on her lower lip. "You don't know that."

"Let's be realistic. We're not you and TJ."

"You guys could be even better."

"Really, Mila?" I laughed. "Is there anything better than you and TJ?"

"Haha, I don't know." She laughed back at me and her eyes were glowing. "I think that would be pretty hard. I mean, we're pretty awesome."

"Yeah, exactly. So if you think you guys are the top, where do me and Cody fit in? We are nowhere on the scale of good. We aren't even on the scale of bad. We aren't even on any scale, that's how pathetic it is."

"Oh Sally." Mila laughed. "Don't say that. That's horrible."

"It's horrible, but true." I started laughing. "It's pathetic.

This whole situation is pathetic. I don't even know why I bother."

"What are you two laughing about?" Cody looked over at me and gave me a curious look.

"Nothing much. Mila was just telling a joke," I said with a smile.

"About me?" TJ raised his eyebrows at me.

"Could it be about anyone or anything else? She's positively obsessed with you."

"That's what I like to hear." He grinned and walked over to us, leaned down and gave Mila a kiss on the cheek. "All you should be talking about and thinking about is me."

"Oh stop with the sap, you two." Cody shook his head as he walked over and joined us. "I hope tonight's not going to be some PDA date-night with your two best friends standing awkwardly at the side."

"Would we do that?" Mila asked him with a small smile.

"Yes." He rolled his eyes. "If I'd known it was going to be some sort of date night, I would have brought a date with me tonight," he said, and my heart sank. I could see Mila's eyes on me and I knew that she knew just how devastated that comment had made me, but I attempted to keep a small smile on my face.

"Yeah, me too. I would have brought one of my guys if I'd known," I lied.

"Oh? What guys?" Cody looked at me. "Anyone I know?"

"No." I shook my head, but inside I was thinking, *How would you know some random guy I was dating?*

"Anyone you're thinking of getting serious with?" he asked again, and I looked at him curiously. Hadn't I just told him ten minutes ago that I wasn't seriously dating anyone? Had he not been paying attention?

"Not really." I shook my head.

"Hey, Cody, Mila and I want to change. Is it okay if we go in your room?" TJ asked as we just stood there.

"Sure." He nodded. "No hanky panky, though."

"Cody." Mila hit him in the shoulder. "You're so disgusting."

"Hey, I know TJ. I wouldn't put anything past him."

"I'm not you." TJ slapped his friend in the arm. "You're the dirty dog in this friendship."

"Haha, you might be right." Cody laughed. "Dude, remember that time in Cancun with those two chicks from Georgia?"

"How can I forget?"

"Should I be hearing about this?" Mila spoke up, looking slightly annoyed.

"Hey, it wasn't me," TJ said innocently. "It was all Cody."

"That, it was." Cody grinned. "That was a fun night." He looked at me. "I won't bore you with the details."

"Thanks," I said, my stomach sinking again. Ugh, I hated hearing stories about Cody with other women. It made me feel so insecure. Knots twisted in my stomach that made me want to throw up.

"Anyway, let's go and change, TJ. We'll be right back, guys." Mila gave me a sympathetic look and they walked out of the room. "We're going to have a great time tonight racing those fast cars around the track."

"Yeah, it'll be fun." I nodded and then I looked at Cody and grinned. "You're going to let me drive first, right?"

"Hmm, not sure." He laughed. "Are you a good driver?"

"I'm an awesome driver." I gave him a look.

"I don't want it to be a bumpy ride." He tilted his head.

"It will be a smooth ride." I rolled my eyes at him and laughed. "I'm a good driver..." I paused as his expression changed. "What?" I looked at him curiously. "What is it you want to say?" I asked again as his eyes grew brighter and he grinned at me.

CHAPTER TWO

Cody

"I CAN TAKE you on the ride of your life. The smoothest ride ever," I said—and then I groaned under my breath, realizing I'd just made a sex joke to my little sister's best friend. I could see her looking at me with wide brown eyes as she waited for me to say something else. Something that would clarify my statement, like, "I'm an awesome driver and I'm great with cars. Let me drive you around first and it will be the ride of your life." Of course, I didn't say that because that wasn't what I'd meant. She knew it and I knew it, so what was the point of pretending? I wasn't even sure why the comment had popped into my mind. Maybe it was because she'd been talking about smooth and bumpy rides and I had a dirty mind. As soon as "ride" had been mentioned, all I could think about was her riding me. Which was highly inappropriate. I knew that. But I was also a guy and always had highly inappropriate thoughts. Even about Sally. Not that I'd ever voiced them before, though.

Normally, I wouldn't care that I'd made a sexual innuendo. Only, that was with girls I didn't know. And that I didn't care about. Sally was different. In a "you're my sister's best friend and I've known you forever" kind of way. I'm the kind of guy who always gets the girl. Well, at least the majority of the time. I'm also the kind of guy that most girls would call smooth. I'm not going to pretend that I'm not. I'm handsome. Some women call me adorable, some call me hot, many call me sexy. I can't help it if I've been blessed. Only, there are times when I'm not so smooth, not so confident, not so self-assured. It doesn't happen often, but sometimes, like right now, I said something that was out of place and I regretted it.

"Sorry, what?" Sally asked, a half-smile on her face. "The ride of my life, huh? What sort of ride could that possibly be?"

"Sleep with me and you'll see," I said teasingly, continuing to go down a road I wasn't sure I should be going down. I laughed to show her that I wasn't being serious, though to be honest, I wasn't really joking. If she said yes, I'd have her in my bedroom in ten seconds flat. Once TJ and Mila exited, of course.

"What did you say?" The smile on Sally's face was shocked and slightly unsure. Her brown eyes looked into mine with a confused expression and I burst out laughing as I gazed at her.

"I'm joking," I said with a huge grin, trying to pretend that I didn't really want to rip her clothes off then and there. She chewed on her lower lip and continued to look at me uncertainly. I wanted to lean forward and take her lower lip in my mouth and suck on it. Only, I knew that wasn't appropriate, though I wasn't sure how appropriate I wanted to be. I'd been appropriate with her our whole lives, so why couldn't I have some fun with her now? We were both adults, after all.

"Oh, okay." She looked at me uncertainly and I worried that maybe I shouldn't be teasing her like this. Maybe it wasn't fair. TJ had told me once that he thought Sally had a crush on me, but I didn't really see it. She'd never tried to hook up with me and I was pretty sure she saw me as a brother. Granted, there had been times when I'd seen her looking at me and batting her eyes, but what did that mean, really? She knew I wasn't the sort of guy who was looking for a girlfriend, so I was sure she would take my flirting innocently. And if she happened to be down for some no-strings-attached sex, who was I to say no? I mean, if I was completely honest with myself, I'd known it when she had a teenage crush on me, but that had seemed to die as soon as it started. And maybe sometimes I wondered if she still liked me. And maybe sometimes I wondered what she was doing and if she was dating anyone, but that didn't mean anything. It didn't mean I wanted anything from her, aside from some hot sex. And hot sex was not worth risking the friendship or the dynamic we had. And Mila would kill me if I hurt her best friend.

"Sorry, that was inappropriate. I shouldn't have gone there." I gave her my most apologetic smile and bowed my head. "But you know us guys, sometimes we don't think properly."

"That's okay." She nodded and gave me a small smile, her face still looking confused.

"But yeah, you can drive first," I said to her, trying to diffuse the situation. "I'm sure you'll be good and if you're not, I can show you how it's done."

"Uh huh." She laughed and shook her head. "Sure you can."

"Sure he can what?" Mila walked back into the room and looked at us curiously.

"I was saying I don't need his help driving a car quickly," Sally said and laughed, throwing her head back, and I watched as her long black hair moved back and forth. She looked at Mila and then she looked at me, her brown eyes gazing into mine softly for a few seconds as she laughed and I was struck at how innocent and youthful she looked. Something in me stirred as I watched her face, and I smiled back at her, unable to stop myself from sharing in her happy moment.

"Oh yeah, don't let Cody drive." Mila laughed and I watched as Sally looked away from me and at her, and the moment was broken. I felt a sense of loss for a few seconds and frowned. I wasn't sure what that was about.

"I think I need to eat," I said and rubbed my stomach. "My head is feeling funny due to lack of food."

"I'm hungry myself," Mila agreed and rubbed her stomach too. "What are we eating? Chinese?"

"No Chinese tonight." Sally shook her head. "What about Indian?"

"I had Indian last night." I shook my head. "What about Thai?"

"We had Thai last night." Mila laughed. "What about Italian?"

"I can do Italian," Sally said, and I grinned.

"Can you now?" I winked at her and she blushed.

"Cody!" Mila growled at me and laughed. "That was so inappropriate."

"I'm an inappropriate guy." I shrugged. "What can I say?"

"If you say you're an Italian stallion, I will slap you." Mila glared at me and I opened my mouth and winked at her.

"I'm an Italian…" I paused and looked at Sally. "Well, maybe one day you'll find out."

"Cody." Sally's face went bright red and I watched as she started fiddling with her hair. Her nails were painted a bright red and I was curious as to whether her toenails were painted the same hue—so bright and flirty.

"Yes?" I said with a wink and she just shook her head. I could see Mila and TJ looking at me and I turned to them with a huge grin, knowing I was going to have to answer some questions later if I didn't slow it down right away. "I'm just joking, guys. Seriously, jeez." I shook my head and pulled out my phone. "Now, let's get going, I've got to make some calls to some ladies tonight."

CHAPTER THREE

Sally

"HOW DID YOU know TJ was your soul mate?" I asked Mila, my best friend, as we waited for TJ and Cody to grab our drinks from the bar. The car racing had been fun and I'd thoroughly enjoyed teasing Cody before our races. His eyes had sparkled as we'd joked around and I'd thought we really had a connection. Only then I'd noticed his eyes following a hot blonde every time she walked past us and my heart had sunk in jealousy. I'd tried to keep a smile on my face, instead of letting my sadness show. I mean, what sort of loser would I be if I expressed my jealousy to him? He'd think I was crazy. Men didn't like jealous women they were in relationships with, let alone jealous women they weren't even dating. And just because I'd thought he'd been flirting earlier didn't mean anything. Because maybe that was just his way and it didn't actually mean anything to him.

"I'm not sure." She shook her long blond hair and looked at me with a tentative smile. "Are you asking me because you want to know about me and TJ or because you want to know about you and Cody?"

"You're too smart." I laughed at my best friend and leaned my head back on the red leather couch. I was surprised at how comfortable the seating was in the bar. I was used to cheap plastic and vinyl and this was a pleasant change. "Why can you always read my mind?"

"Because I'm in your mind." She handed me a bottle of water from her bag and sat next to me. "Plus I was in your shoes just a few months ago. Drink this while we wait for the boys to bring our drinks."

"Water?"

"I know how you get when you drink too much." She nodded. "We don't need you telling Cody anything you'll regret in the morning."

"True," I agreed and opened the bottle of water and took a sip. "I shouldn't get drunk. I'll either tell him I love him or that I hate him, and neither of those statements sound like a good idea."

"Yeah, no." Mila laughed and I watched as she rested her head back and smiled at me. She had such a look of contentment on her face and as I smiled back at her, I realized just how much I envied her peace of mind and happiness. And that made me feel horrible. I loved Mila. She was my best friend and I wanted nothing but the best for her, but seeing how happy she was with TJ sometimes made me feel like my own life was even more of a mess. I felt like I was living in daydreams. I wanted so much to be with Cody that every little smile he gave me meant something more than it did. I needed to get out of my head, but I just didn't know how to do that.

"I know how hard it is, Sally." Mila gave me a sympathetic smile and stared at me for a few seconds. "It's such a mentally exhausting position to be in. I've been there."

"Yeah, but now you're engaged to Mr. Wonderful and I'm just here still wondering what I'm doing wrong with my life." I sighed before taking a large gulp of water, wishing it were wine. "Am I wasting my time waiting around for Cody?"

"Is that what you're doing?" Mila asked me softly. "Waiting around?" She looked at me hesitantly, her eyes soft as she looked into mine. She looked beautiful, but I always found that the glow of love gave you something makeup never could.

"I don't know." I shook my head. "It sounds stupid to say I'm waiting around on someone who might never love me. Might never want me. It sounds pitiful."

"You're not pitiful." Mila grabbed my hands and squeezed them together. "You're the man."

"Only, I'm not a man." I made a rueful smile at her and laughed. "I'm a woman. A woman desperately in love with a man who doesn't even know I exist."

"He knows you exist." Mila laughed, but she stopped laughing within seconds as she surveyed my face. "Are you okay? And before you answer, let's go to the bar and grab the bottle of wine that the bartender just gave the guys."

"I'm fine." I sighed a long, deep, dark sigh. "I'll be fine," I said and followed her back to the bar, trying to still the excitement in my heart as we neared Cody.

"We can always come up with a plan," Mila said thoughtfully, her eyes sparkling as we walked. "I can't say it will work, but maybe."

"A plan?" I asked her curiously. "What sort of plan?"

"I thought you'd never ask." She grinned at me and then lowered her voice. "Hold on, I'll tell you more when we get back to the table." She winked at me and we stopped next to the guys. "Hey, we'll take the bottle now, thank you." She grinned at TJ, who looked at her lovingly and I just stood there, avoiding eye contact with Cody.

"You girls don't want to wait here at the bar with us?" Cody said teasingly and I looked over at him. His eyes were on me and I shook my head and smiled. He winked at me then, a slow teasing wink and I couldn't stop my heart from fluttering. Why was he such a flirt?

"I think we'll wait at the table for you guys," I said finally. "We'd rather sit than stand, thank you very much."

"You can sit on my lap if you want," Cody said and winked again, and my mind went to all sorts of naughty places. "There's a barstool." He nodded at it and grinned at me.

"I think I could just sit on the stool directly as opposed to your lap," I retorted, and he laughed.

"What fun would that be?" he said, and my face flushed as he continued to stare at me.

"I'm not sure either way would be fun," I said, and he nodded with a sly smile.

"Touché." He handed me two wine glasses and I looked over at Mila, who was staring at us curiously.

"You ready?" I asked her before she could tell Cody to stop playing with me.

"Yeah." She nodded and I watched as TJ leaned over and gave her a kiss on the cheek. She smiled up at him happily and then started walking toward our booth. I followed behind her and we stood next to the booth. I handed her the wine glasses as we stood there.

"Let's sit down." She grinned at me as she poured me a large glass of red wine. "You're going to need to be sitting down for this."

"So what's this brilliant plan you have, then?" I asked Mila, my mind wondering if she actually had a good solution, a way for me to get Cody without feeling like a fool. I was slightly hopeful that she'd have a good idea. I mean, she had gotten TJ, after all.

"Well, I don't know that I would call it brilliant. It's not like I'm the queen of love, or cupid, but I think it's a good idea," she said as she filled her glass as well.

"How good?" I asked her curiously, my mind wondering. She wasn't going to tell me to go back up to the bar to give Cody a lap dance or something, was she? I grinned to myself as I imagined the look of shock on Cody's face if I were to do such a thing. I wondered if he would enjoy it. If he'd get excited. If I'd get excited. I took a quick sip of wine to stop myself from thinking such crazy thoughts. There was no way in hell I was going to go to the bar to give Cody a lap dance.

"Well, let me get it out and I'll tell you. Come, let's sit down." She grabbed my arm and pulled me into the booth next to her.

"Why do I have to be sitting down? It's not completely crazy, is it?" I sat back into the comfy couch and took another sip, looking back at the bar and staring at Cody's ass. His jeans looked so snug and tight on his athletic legs. He was just so sexy. "You don't want me to give him a lap dance, do you? Because that would be absolutely crazy."

"Don't be silly, Sally. When have I ever suggested you do something crazy?" Mila laughed slightly after she spoke.

"Plenty of times." I shook my head. "Just as I've suggested plenty of crazy ideas to you. Ideas that you've actually done."

"You're braver than me," she started and gave me a huge grin. "And, plus, this idea isn't crazy, I promise."

"Do I need to gulp my glass of wine down before you talk?" I glanced at her. "Hmm?"

"No." She grinned. "But if you think it will help, yes."

"Okay, fine," I said and sipped on it slowly. "Hit me. What is it?"

"What is it? Just the most brilliant plan I've ever had."

"Hmmm," I said and pursed my lips, not fully convinced. "Let me hear it, then."

"You know how they say that you should date your best friend—?"

"Hold up." I put my hand up. "I'm not interested in dating you, Mila." I fake glared at her and she burst out laughing.

"No, silly, not me."

"I'm not getting into any girl-on-girl action either. I'm not interested in that." I glared at her again, wondering if she had lost her head. "That is not a good idea. I'm not going to be one of those girls who tries to titillate a guy by pretending to be interested in girls. That's worse than the lap-dance idea."

"Sally, I didn't say anything about girls." Mila's face was bemused. "And you're the one who brought up lap dancing, not me. Just listen to me."

"I'm listening." I gave her a small eye roll.

"I want you to listen and not interrupt me. You can talk at the end, okay?"

"Fine." I sighed. "Go ahead."

"Okay, so here's the deal." She sat back sipping her wine slowly, and I stared at the huge diamond engagement ring on her finger. It sparkled and I felt my heart swelling in happiness for my best friend. She'd been in love with TJ for so long and it had seemed like such a long shot that he would be interested in her. Even I had doubted he had any real interest in her. Yet, it had all worked out. Maybe Mila really did know something about love, or maybe she had just gotten lucky. Either way, she was my best bet at figuring out how to get Cody to show some real attention to me and not just the innocent idle flirtation.

"I'm listening," I said, my heart starting to race nervously.

"So, like I said, I think you should date and marry your best friend."

"Yeah." I nodded. "I heard that part. So exactly what is the plan? You haven't said anything past that."

"So, Cody needs to become your best friend." She leaned forward expectantly, waiting for me to respond. I stared back at her, waiting for her to say something else. Only she didn't continue talking.

"Cody needs to become my best friend?" I repeated after her, confused. "Just exactly how does that happen?"

"That's where the plan comes into place." She grinned at him. "Essentially, you worm your way into his life. Get closer and closer to him as friends. You're going to friend-zone him."

"Eh, why would I friend-zone him if I actually want him?"

"Because guys always want someone they can't have." She nodded, her mind obviously working overtime. "And, well, guys don't respect friend zones. He's not going to be like 'oh I'm in the friend zone, I will never try and hit on her'. He's going to be like, 'shit, this girl is hot, I want her, who cares about the friend zone?'"

"Um, I don't know about that. Aren't I already in the friend zone? Isn't it pretty obvious that I've been interested in him for a long time? And he certainly hasn't disrespected any of my boundaries yet."

"Yeah, he probably knows you've been interested in him for some amount of time, or were interested at one time, but guess what, it's easy to get out of that. Guys don't overanalyze like we do. All you need is to have another guy around, someone else interested in you, throw it in his face, not overtly, but maybe you can ask him for guy advice, relationship advice sort of stuff. That way you show him you're over him and into other guys and he's the one who's now friend-zoned."

"But that's not true." I frowned. "And where am I getting these other guys from? It's not like they're swarming around me."

"You join some online dating sites, plus we'll go to bars."

"TJ will be cool with that?" I asked her with a raised eyebrow. TJ was a confident, cocky man, but he was always jealous when Mila was around other men. I couldn't see him being happy with her going out with me to pick up other men. "Also, are you going to tell TJ that this is a game for me, meeting these other guys? That I'm trying to make Cody jealous? What if TJ tells Cody? How embarrassing would that be?"

"I'm not going to tell TJ." She shook her head. "At least not now. I don't think he would tell Cody, though." Mila looked thoughtful. "I'll just tell him that you want to meet some new guys and need a friend with you."

"Yeah, he might not tell him on purpose, but what if something slipped out, like, 'Damn, that Sally is really into you, she's playing all these games to get to you.'"

"TJ would never let something like that slip." Mila shook her head and laughed. "That wouldn't be an innocent slip. And I'm not going to tell him it's all a game. Not at first, anyway. But I will eventually, since TJ is my fiancé and I don't want to lie to him. Plus, he's a good guy. You can trust him."

"Yeah, well, TJ's not really an innocent, is he?" I raised an eyebrow at her. "I mean, before you guys got together, he was a jackass to both of us." I laughed. "He was always making fun of us. And this is something I can imagine him making fun of me for."

"That's just his way." Mila looked at me with a small, loving smile, though I knew she was thinking of TJ's ways much more affectionately now than I was. I didn't love him.

"Exactly." I gave her a pointed look. "That's his way. He's not just going to stop doing it. Yeah, maybe he's going to stop teasing you because he loves you and he wants to marry you and keep having sex with you." I laughed at the look on her face. "But nothing has changed with me. He's still going to keep teasing me. And if I'm going to do this crazy plan and try and get Cody to be my BFF, then I'm not going to want to be worried that TJ is going to let something slip and make me look like an idiot."

"So you're entertaining the idea?" Mila said with a smile, ignoring my TJ disses.

"Maybe. I don't know." I sighed. "It doesn't seem like the worst idea. And then at least I'd get to spend time with him, so even if he didn't fall in love with me, he'd still be in my life." I took another sip of wine. "Oh God, I sound pathetic, don't I?"

"Not pathetic. You just sound like someone who wants to be around the man you love."

"I can't really love him though, can I?" I groaned and placed the glass of wine down on the table in front of me. "This is just sad. I'm in love with a guy who sees me only as his sister's best friend and now I'm trying to become his best friend so I can be closer to him, so that I can hopefully make him jealous and get him to fall in love with me."

"We can't help who we love." Mila shrugged. "That's why I got into the fake engagement with TJ. I just wanted to spend time with him. I mean, that wasn't the best situation for me in any way. I thought my heart was going to be ripped out of my chest. I thought my soul was going to leave my body forever."

"Yeah, but it worked out for you." I gave her a weak smile. "And, well, TJ at least was eager to sleep with you. Cody has never given me any real indication that he's interested in anything with me. No dating, no kissing, no bending me over a bed and taking me. He's not given me any indication for anything. And I know he's not asexual."

"Would you be happy if he tried to make a move, like he did with Barbie?" Mila said softly. "Honestly, how would you have felt? What if he basically had a one-night stand with you and then never spoke to you again?"

"Well, I'd feel like shit, but at least I'd know that he'd at least been attracted to me once." I gave her a wry smile.

"Sex isn't even always about attraction," Mila said. "Plus, Cody's an idiot—one of those guys who gets drunk enough and sleeps with anyone."

"Well, Barbie wasn't exactly ugly," I said as I thought about the girl Cody had slept with a few months ago at Mila's lake house. My heart had ripped in two when I realized they'd hooked up. Barbie was beautiful—one of those girls that every girl is jealous of. She made me feel so insecure, with her perfect body and perfect looks. And the fact that her personality was awful had only made things worse because it made me realize that personality really accounted for nothing. She'd been the biggest bitch, yet that hadn't stopped Cody from hooking up with her the first chance he got. I didn't even care that he'd been drunk. In fact, part of me wanted to write him off completely. He obviously had no feelings for me, if he was able to do that. Absolutely no feelings at all.

The emptiness that resounded through my body made me feel so hopeless and lost. All I could think was *What's the point?* What was the point of allowing myself to dream of him when there was never going to be anything between us? If I didn't even matter to him one iota. But the hope in me wouldn't die, especially after Mila and TJ got together. I figured maybe I had a chance. Maybe Cody would one day wake up and think to himself, "Oh shit, look, here's Sally. She's been here all along. I love her more than anything in my life. I want her so bad. I need to be with her. She's my soul mate. The love of my life. How can I live without her?" It was a longshot, but it was worth a try. I sighed loudly as I looked at Mila. Her eyes crinkled as she stared at me, and she gave me a half-smile.

"You okay?" She reached over and patted my hand.

"Not really," I said and took a deep breath. "How can I be okay when I don't even know if I'm coming or going? How can I be okay when I don't know if the sun is even shining? How can I be okay when all I think about is him, day and night? Even my dreams are pervaded with him. He's on my mind all the time. He distracts me at the gym, when I'm reading a book, when I'm watching TV. He distracts me right now and I'm talking about him. I don't know what to do, Mila. I think I'm going crazy. I know I'm obsessed. I know this isn't healthy. I just don't know what I should do. Should I just give up? Should I go to a mental asylum? Should I seek professional help?"

"Sally." Mila started laughing. "You don't need to go to a mental asylum. You're not crazy. I know how you feel, though. I was there with TJ. It's hard to know when to give up. But you have to ask yourself one question."

"What's that?" I said, slightly annoyed she was laughing, but understanding how dramatic I sounded.

"Do you want to be with him?"

"That's a stupid question." I rolled my eyes at her. "Of course I want to be with him."

"No, I mean, is that the most important thing in your life? Do you think you're meant to be with him? Do you want to be with him for the rest of your life? Do you think he's perfect? Do you see him as your soulmate? Forget your emotions. The love in your heart. Forget the years you've been wanting him. Forget everything you think you know. Now clear your brain. Think of him. Just Cody. As a person. Forget his looks. Think about how he treats you. How he treats me. Think about what he does for a living. His interests. If he loves dogs, kids, how he treats elderly people, the foods he likes to eat, the jokes he makes. Think about the good and the bad. Can you deal with that? Is he the man you want?"

"Yes." I nodded simply. "Even the bad things are things I love. Do I sound pathetic?"

"You do know he cuts his toenails in the living room and leaves the clippings on the table?" Mila asked me softly. "And I'm sure he rarely does laundry."

"Mila!" I laughed and shook my head.

"I'm not lying." She laughed. "I've seen him in the same outfit five days in one week and I know it's the same clothes and not just duplicates, because I've seen the same stains on the clothes day in and day out and sometimes he smells." She made a face. "Granted, he doesn't do that every week. If he did, there would be a major intervention, but I'm not sure he showers every day either."

"Mila, are you trying to turn me off of him?" I looked at her and laughed. "These are not the best qualities that you're bringing up."

"I just wanna make sure this isn't about the fantasy of Cody."

"Trust me, I know how gross he is." I laughed. "You and I have been best friends for years, remember? I've known him for ages. I remember when he really didn't shower for weeks. Remember that time in high school?" I made a face. "Your mom and dad threw that bucket of water over him?"

"And Nonno held the hose up to him." She nodded, her face nostalgic. "That was hilarious. Nonno said if he was going to act like a dog, he would get washed like a dog."

"Yeah, that was funny." I nodded. "Nonno was hilarious."

"Yeah. I miss him," Mila said with a soft smile and my heart ached for her, as her Nonno had passed away recently. It had been a shock to everyone in the family, but especially to Mila. Mila and her Nonno had had such a close relationship and she'd been devastated when he died. But he'd left her the greatest gift he could have. He left her with a relationship that she'd wanted forever. It had been Nonno who had really been instrumental in getting her together with TJ. I wished I had a Nonno who could do something like that for me, but I guess I'd just have to rely on Mila's help. "Anyway, let's think how to get this started," Mila said softly.

"How to get what started?" I asked, confused at the sudden change of subject.

"How to get you and Cody as best friends." She grinned.

"Oh that, so we're doing it?" I chewed on my lower lip nervously. "Do you really think this is a good idea?"

"Yeah, it's a great idea." She nodded. "Okay, maybe not great, but I think it's pretty solid. Right?" She looked at me uncertainly.

"Girl, I have no idea." I laughed. "I obviously have no ideas, or I wouldn't be sitting here entertaining yours."

"Okay, so we go with Plan A, then." She grinned.

"Is it really Plan A if there is no Plan B?" I laughed.

"Shh. Stop being a pessimist."

"I'm not a pessimist, I'm a realist. And honestly, I don't know how this is going to work. But I'm a sucker and a loser and if it means I get to spend more time with Cody, then I'll do it. I guess it's a nice consolation prize. We can be best friends, even if we're not going to be living together happily ever after."

"And hey, maybe best friends is better, right? Best friends are for life, whereas relationships can end. I mean, this could mean that you guys can be together forever."

"Huh?"

"I mean, be together in each other's lives forever. Always enjoying a close relationship. Maybe you'll be his closest confidante."

"Uhm, yeah." I made a face. "I guess that's true."

"He'll call you before he calls anyone else. You'll grab dinners on Fridays. Talk on the phone every Sunday. Your families will spend vacations together. You'll be old and gray together, talking about how great your friendship is."

"Yeah." I frowned slightly and gave her a look, my stomach sinking at her words. "Uhm you do know that I don't just want to be his best friend, right? I mean, yeah that would be cool, but frankly I think it would kill me to be spending Friday dinners with him, knowing his wife was at home with his kids. That is not the consolation prize I want. I'd rather kill myself than have that life."

"I know that's not the goal, but if that's what happens, are you okay with that?" Mila looked over at the bar and stared at Cody for a few seconds and then back at me, her expression thoughtful.

"Mila, the friendship would be over so fast if that were to happen. There is no way in hell that I can see us as best friends and me being cool with his wife and kids and not feeling jealous as hell." I groaned and put my face in my hands. "Honestly, it would kill me. It makes me want to cry right now, just thinking of him with someone else."

"Well, you'd be married with your own kids as well."

"I, yeah, uhm, if that's the way you think this is going to go down, then maybe this isn't such a good idea. That's not the end goal I'm looking for." I grabbed my glass and took another large sip of wine.

"I mean, yeah, that's not the ultimate goal." She looked guilty. "I'm not even sure why I brought that up. That's not an option. The goal is for you and Cody to get married."

"Or to date, at least. I at least want a chance for him to really get to know me and see if he wants to be with me. I want him to fall in love with me."

"Our main goal should be the end goal though, right?" Mila looked at me hesitantly. "I mean, the end goal isn't to go on a few dates, is it? I mean, what's a few dates? If what you say is true and he's the love of your life... If he's the one you want to spend the rest of your life with... If he's the one you think about, the one you love, the one in your heart... Then he's the one you want to spend eternity with. He's the one you want to marry."

"I just feel like a psycho saying that out loud." I made a face at her. "We haven't even kissed and I want to marry him? How does that not sound crazy?"

"Hey, we all need to be a little crazy." She grinned. "And if that's what you want, you need to call it into being."

"Call it into being? Oh my God Mila, what are you talking about?"

"You need to create a vision board."

"A vision board?" I blinked at her. "What's that?"

"It's a board of what you envision in your life. What you want to accomplish. What you see in your future."

"Uhm, okay?"

"So we need to get your favorite photo of Cody and put it front and center."

"What?" I screeched. "I'm not putting a photo of Cody on a board. That really is psycho."

"Sally, listen to me."

"Ugh, I'm afraid to keep listening." I laughed. "This is getting crazier by the second." I put the glass back down on the table and put my face in my hands and groaned. "And the crazier *you* get, the crazier *I'm* going to get."

"What's going on, girls?" TJ drawled as he approached the table with Cody close behind him. TJ held a pitcher of beer in his hands and Cody held two mugs.

"Not much," I squeaked out as my eyes flew open and my face grew red. I tried to think about how loud my voice had been, but I was pretty sure that TJ and Cody hadn't overheard our conversation.

"What do you guys want to do next?" Cody asked, chugging down his beer. "I know this cool place on 8th Street—they have a mechanical bull."

"A mechanical bull?" Mila peered at him as she spoke. "Are we expected to get on the bull?"

"Nah." He shook his head. "But we can always go and watch."

"Cody." Mila sighed and rolled her eyes. "That doesn't sound like fun."

"It's plenty fun." He laughed and licked his lips. "What I wouldn't do to be that bull."

"Cody." Mila shook her head and looked at me with a rueful smile. "Guys!"

"Yeah." I tried to laugh nonchalantly, like I thought it was funny that Cody wanted to go and ogle some random girls. "You're a pig, Cody." I looked at him and he laughed, his eyes wide and happy as he stared at me.

"What can I say?" He grinned and winked at me. My insides fluttered at his smile and I wanted to smack myself. Why did he have such an effect on me? Just one smile and my insides were turned to jelly. How I wanted to turn off the switch inside of me that responded to his every glance and smile. Where was the off switch when I needed it?

"You can say what you want, but that won't change what we already think and know," I shot back at him and winked.

"You think you know, but you don't really know," Cody said with a twist of his lips, his hazel eyes bright with mirth as he chugged down his beer.

"Oh, I know." I laughed, surprised at how carefree I felt. "Trust me, I know."

"We all know," Mila added and punched her brother in the shoulder.

"What are they even talking about?" Cody asked TJ, who just shook his head.

"I have no clue." He sipped on his beer and laughed. "But then, I never really have a clue."

"So we're going to go to ride some bulls?" Cody asked eagerly, and we all just looked at each other and burst out laughing. I looked over at Mila, who was studying my face, and I gave her a small nod. I was down to try her plan. I loved Cody. I wanted to get to know Cody better. And if this was the way to get into his life on a deeper level, I was going to take my chance. I was going to go big, and if it didn't work out, I'd just go home.

CHAPTER FOUR

Cody

"SO HOW ABOUT them bulls?" I chugged down the last of my beer and grinned at TJ as he and Mila and Sally waited for me so we could leave the bar.

"How about 'em?" TJ grinned at me and I lifted up my hand to high-five him. I saw Mila glaring at him from the corner of my eye, but I was too buzzed to care.

"That was frigging awesome," I called out to the hot redhead who was walking past. She looked over at me with a big smile and licked her lips slowly, seductively. "You sure know how to ride those bulls," I said again and winked at her.

"I know how to ride a lot of things." She paused and ran her fingers down the valley between her breasts. "I like to ride."

"Oh, really?" I said, about to take a step closer to her.

"Cody." Mila's voice was sharp. "Really?" she snapped at me and I glanced over at her. Her face was pissed and then I looked at Sally, who had turned away from me, and TJ who was shaking his head slightly. I put my hands up in the air and laughed and then looked back at the sexy redhead.

"Well, have a good night riding." I grinned at her. "I think we're about to leave."

"Pity," the redhead said and sucked on one of her fingers. "We could have had some fun." She tossed her hair and then walked away.

"Thanks for nothing, Mila." I rolled my eyes at my sister and then looked at Sally, who was still avoiding my gaze. "Sally…" I said her name slowly. "Sally," I said again, wanting her attention.

"Yes, Cody?" she said, as she finally looked at me.

"Nothing." I laughed. "Wanna get another drink?"

"No, I'm okay, thanks."

"Come on." I reached over and grabbed her hand. "Let's get a drink and dance."

"I think we're all ready to go home now, Cody." TJ gave me one of his looks. I tried not to roll my eyes at him. Ever since he got serious with Mila, he'd started becoming more and more like my dad and had lost almost all of his fun.

"I'm not ready." I shook my head. "Are you ready, Sally?"

"Kinda," she said.

"Let's go, Cody," Mila said, frowning as she looked at me. "We've watched enough people riding bulls. I don't think we need to watch people dancing now."

"I don't want to watch people dancing. I want to dance. With Sally." I pulled her toward me and spun her around. "We can two-step, or salsa, or even bump-n-grind. I'm not picky."

"You can't even dance." Mila rolled her eyes at me.

"I can dance when I'm drunk enough." I started moving slowly and pulled Sally closer to me. She stumbled slightly against me and I held her close to me for a few seconds. "You okay?"

"Yeah." She blinked up at me and grinned. "I'm fine."

"Good," I said softly, gazing down into her big beautiful brown eyes.

"So show me your dance moves, then," she said softly, not moving back.

"Is that a challenge?" I stared at her lips for a few seconds, enjoying the feel of her body next to mine.

"I just want to see your moves," she said, moving back and forth slowly. "Can you keep up with me?"

"Hmm, let me see." I put my hands on her waist and started moving my hips against her.

"Okay, guys. I think we're going to go." TJ looked over at me and I could see him smiling at me slightly. "You guys okay to get home?"

"Yeah, we'll catch a cab. I'll make sure Sally gets home safely."

"You sure you want to stay and dance, Sally?" Mila asked her friend, and I felt myself waiting with bated breath to see what she was going to say.

"Sure, why not?" She laughed, throwing her head back, her hair flying past my face as she moved. I grinned at her and pulled her closer to me.

"You two boring folks go home, we're going to continue having fun."

"I guess," Mila said, chewing her lower lip, looking slightly nervous. "Sally, we can all ride together, if you want?"

"I'm cool," Sally said as she looked at Mila. "I'm just going to enjoy the night."

"Okay." Mila nodded, then turned towards TJ. "Let's go, then. I'm tired. I'll see you both in a few days, yeah?"

"Sounds good. Bye, Sis." I smiled at her and then watched as she and TJ left. I leaned down and whispered in Sally's ear as we moved to the beat of the rock music that was playing in the bar. "Wanna grab another drink here or do you want to hit a different bar?"

"I don't mind." She shrugged, looking up at me with a small smile. "What do you want to do?" she asked me softly. I stared down at her face and at her lips again and pulled her to me roughly, enjoying the feel of her breasts against my chest.

"I want to do whatever you want me to do," I said, leaning down so that my lips were a mere centimeter from hers. My hands fell to her ass and I squeezed her butt-cheeks as I brought her closer. She gasped then, her lips falling open as her eyes widened and I pressed my lips down against hers for a brief second before alarm bells started going off in my head. What was I doing? I was making a huge mistake and I could see from Sally's eyes that she was feeling confused as well. I pulled back from her abruptly and let go of her. She stumbled back slightly, looking confused, and I started laughing to lighten the mood. "Gotcha." I grinned at her. "Let's go find a cab. I think I need to go home and sleep." I looked at my watch. "I have to get up early tomorrow."

"Oh, okay." She looked at me with more confusion and maybe a hint of disappointment. I knew I wasn't making sense to her and I knew I was being slightly rude, but I didn't know what else to do. I was too drunk to make smart decisions and Sally wasn't the girl to be making bad decisions with.

"Come." I grabbed her hand. "Let's go," I said and pulled her toward the entrance. "I promise I will get you home safely."

"Thanks," she said softly. "I appreciate it." Her voice trailed off as we pushed past the crowds of people and I could feel my body burning up as we exited the bar.

CHAPTER FIVE

Sally

"SO IS MILA here yet?" I looked around the living room and gave Cody a questioning look. It was 9 a.m. and I'd just arrived at his house according to the plan that Mila and I had come up with. I felt like a bit of a fool and I was really hoping my acting job was going to work out well. Especially after our near kiss from a few nights ago. I didn't want him figuring out that I wanted him any way I could have him.

"Nope, not yet." He shook his head and yawned, stretching his arms up, and I tried not to stare at his naked chest.

"I guess she and TJ are running behind?" I said again, pretending like I didn't know they weren't even going to show up. I felt my face warming up as I stood there lying my ass off. Who knew this was going to be so hard?

"Yeah, you know Mila." He nodded and then pointed at the couch. "You can sit down, if you want."

"Thanks." I nodded and made my way to the couch and sat. He walked over to me and plopped down next to me.

"Sorry, I should have showered already." He grinned at me as he ran his hands through his hair. "I had a late night last night."

"Oh?" I smiled at him uncertainly, not really wanting to know what he'd been doing the previous evening. Though it struck me that he'd slept the night in his apartment and it didn't appear as if there was anyone else here, so that most likely meant that he hadn't hooked up with anyone. Unless of course he'd gone back to their place and then left early in the morning. Or unless he'd hooked up while out, or…I forced myself to stop thinking of the possibilities. Jealousy was not going to help me in this situation. Especially seeing as I didn't even know if I had anything to be jealous about.

"I got in late. Went to a concert with some friends and then we went gambling." He grinned. "Too many free drinks."

"Where did you guys go gambling?" I asked curiously, happy that he'd been with guys. Or at least I assumed he'd been with guys.

"If I told you, I'd have to kill you." He winked at me and sat back. I looked at his smiling face and felt my heart expanding with love. Why did he have to be so handsome? Why did I react to his every smile as if it were made just for me?

"An illegal gambling place?" I raised an eyebrow at him and he laughed and winked again.

"Not saying." He licked his lips and then ran his hands down his thighs. I found my eyes staring at his thick tan muscular thighs, and I swallowed hard. Not only was he handsome, he was super fit, and I could feel my whole body tingling as I glanced at him. All he was wearing was a pair of navy blue boxers and I was having a hard time keeping my hands to myself. I just wanted to reach out and touch his legs or his chest. Just to see if they felt as magical as they looked. "Hey, you thirsty?" he asked me curiously. "You want a coffee or tea or something?"

"Uhm, maybe some water, please?" I smiled. I needed to text Mila and figure out what I should do next. My mind had gone to mush and I had already forgotten the plan. I mean, phase one was in effect. Cody thought we were all meeting up to discuss the wedding. But Mila and TJ weren't going to show up. This would give us time alone together. However, I felt like we'd already hit a snag in the plan. Cody was barely out of bed. I was barely coherent and I had no clue what I was going to say we should do once he realized Mila and TJ weren't coming.

"Sure." He jumped up. "You hungry? You want anything to eat?"

"I'm okay," I said. I was way too nervous to eat, but then I groaned because I realized that I should have told him I was hungry because then maybe we could have gone out to eat somewhere.

"Okay," He nodded. "I'm not sure what I have in my kitchen so that's probably a good thing."

"Why offer me a bite if you have no food?" I laughed at him.

"I was trying to be polite." He grinned back. "Come with me to the kitchen and then I'll hop in the shower real quick."

"Okay." I nodded, wanting to say that I could hop in with him and wash his back. But of course I didn't. I wasn't that forward. At least not with him. I'd lost all my confidence and mojo with him. I was so scared I was going to mess something up or that he was going to reject me. But the hardest part, the part that made everything worse, was the not knowing. Not knowing if I even had a chance. Not knowing if he cared at all. Not knowing if he fancied me. I bit my lip for a second as doubt came crashing in. Did I really not know, though? Wouldn't he have made a move if he was interested? I mean, generally that's what guys did. I knew that. There were many Tom, Dick, and Harrys who had tried to get my attention. Men I hadn't been interested in. That was always the way. The ones you didn't want, wanted you. I didn't know what to think. I wanted him to want me. Yet, in my heart of hearts it felt like a pipe dream. All the articles said if a guy liked you then he would make a move.

"Tap water okay?" he asked me as I followed him to the kitchen and he grabbed a glass from the cupboard. "I don't have any bottled water."

"Tap is fine." I nodded. "Is it filtered?"

"I had a Brita once." He shrugged. "I forgot to put it on the faucet."

"Oh, okay."

"It still tastes good though."

"It's fine." I smiled. "A little water won't kill you."

"Maybe in South America or Africa." He gave me a smile. "Cholera and dysentery and all that jazz. Yellow fever."

"Uhm, yeah." I took the glass from him and smiled. "Do you get yellow fever from water?" I asked him curiously. "I'm not a doctor or a medical person or anything, but didn't know that yellow fever was from water."

"To be honest, I have no clue." He shrugged, his eyes crinkling as he looked at me. "Call Mila, will ya? And I'll head in the shower now."

"Okies." I nodded and my stomach dropped as he headed out of the kitchen. What was I going to call Mila and say, and what was I going to say to him when he got out of the shower? This really didn't seem to be going well. I wasn't feeling any interest from Cody. In fact, I was feeling less than no interest. I was almost feeling disinterest. I pursed my lips and tried to ignore the panicky and upset feeling that was swelling through me. I felt like a loser and I didn't understand why. What was it about me that he didn't like? Why did he seem to hook up with so many different women, but I meant nothing to him? My heart thudded as my brain answered, "He's not interested in you." I held on to my glass of water and walked back to the living room and sat down. I reached for the remote control and turned the TV on to try and distract myself from my thoughts. I pulled my phone out of my pocket and responded to Mila's text.

"How's it going?"

"Not good. I'm going to leave. He's not interested."

"Sally, you're not going anywhere. This is only phase one of the operation."

"The operation is doomed to fail."

"Shh."

"Shh what? It's true. He's not interested."

"What happened? Why do you think it's going to fail?"

"Hello! He's just not interested, Mila."

"Right now, you're just trying to be his best friend."

"Dude, we're barely friends. I'm sure he doesn't want to be my best friend."

"Sally. Come on, we talked about this."

"Eh, I think I'm over it. I don't think I can do this."

"You haven't done anything yet."

"I don't think it's going to work."

"It's worth a try."

"Is it really?"

I spoke out loud as I typed. Was this really a good idea? It sounded fun and like some cute rom-com movie I'd watch on TV, but did life ever go like rom-com movies? Not really. I didn't know anyone who was in a relationship after going through some crazy-ass schemes. I mean, even Mila's relationship wasn't exactly the same. She'd known TJ was interested in her from the beginning of their fake relationship, even if just for sex. She'd at least known he desired her and wanted her. Cody didn't even look at me as if he wanted me. He didn't care about me, period.

"Sally, shall I call you?"

"No," I said and then typed. *"I'll call you later."*

I put my phone back in my pocket and then leaned back

into the couch and looked around the living room. Cody had no photos anywhere, which was a little surprising to me. He had four big posters on his wall depicting four different movies: *The Godfather*, *Taxi Driver*, *Rocky*, and *Fight Club*. Everything about the room reminded me that he was a bachelor. Which should have made me happy, I suppose, the fact that he was still single. But I wasn't sure it made me feel any better. He was single and still not interested. It might have been easier for me if he were in a relationship. If he were seeing someone, I would just automatically back off. I'd be able to move on from the crush, and my feelings. Or at least that was what I told myself.

"So any news?" Cody suddenly appeared in the doorway, in just a towel, with his hair and body still wet.

"No." I shook my head and swallowed hard. "Mila says they might not be able to make it after all."

"Oh, okay." He rolled his eyes. "Sounds like Mila."

"Yeah." I laughed, unsure what to say next.

"You sure you're not hungry? Wanna go and grab some breakfast?" He tilted his head to the side and looked at me. "I was thinking of going for pancakes."

"I could always go for pancakes." I smiled, things starting to look up. "Especially if they have blueberries and chocolate chips."

"Gross." He laughed.

"That's not gross." I shook my head, just staring at his chest and a drop of water that was rolling from his pecs down to his stomach.

"Yeah, it is." He grinned and stretched and my eyes widened as his towel slipped slightly. Shit, what if his towel fell off? Whoa, that would be amazing. Awkward, but amazing. "You okay?" he said and he stepped closer to me.

"Yeah, why?" I asked softly as he stopped right in front of

me.

"You have a funny look on your face," he said as he looked down at me, his eyes glittering.

"What do you mean, funny?" I asked and wondered if he knew I was staring at his magnificent body and drooling. *Oh my God, please don't let him know I'm staring at his chest and towel, hoping to see what's beneath the towel.*

CHAPTER SIX

Cody

STOOD IN front of Sally, her mouth slightly open, and I had the wickedest thoughts. I stared at her soft pink lips and all I wanted was to tell her that if she leaned forward, she could put her lips to work. I wanted to groan out loud as I stood there. I wasn't even sure why I'd come over to the couch. Maybe it was the way she looked at me when I walked into the room. She'd been shocked I'd come straight from the shower. I had to admit I wanted to see her reaction, and then when I stretched and my towel slipped, her eyes had widened and I'd almost laughed. She had definitely thought the towel was going to drop and she was going to get a view. I wonder what she would have done? I shook my head slightly. I shouldn't be thinking these thoughts. It was improper. She was Mila's best friend and I'd known her for years. She wasn't like other girls. I couldn't just expect her to get on her knees and pleasure me and be okay with that.

"Hello, earth to Cody?" She jumped up and tapped me on the shoulder. "You okay?" Her big brown eyes glanced into mine.

"Yeah, why?" I could feel heat where she'd touched my skin, her fingers warm and smooth on my skin.

"I asked you a question and you just spaced out." She blinked at me. "So I wanted to make sure you were okay."

"I was just thinking about your horrible taste in breakfast foods." I winked at her and she laughed. I grinned then, and reached over and brushed a piece of hair away from her eyes, unable to stop myself. "Sorry, you had hair in your eyes," I said to her as she stared at my hands in a confused way. "I didn't want you to get blinded."

"Thanks for thinking of me," she said with a small smile and she took a step back. I thought about really trying to shock her, but then decided not to. Why play with fire? If there was only one woman in the world who was off-limits, that wasn't so bad. I knew Mila would kill me if I messed around with Sally and then moved on. That would just be awkward for all of us. Plus, I knew Sally'd had a crush on me when we were younger. I wasn't sure if she did anymore, but I knew I wasn't looking for anything serious. There would be nothing worse than us hooking up and then her expecting something I wasn't willing to give.

"Any time." I nodded and stepped back. "Okay, I'm going to go and change."

"Okay," she said and sat back on the couch. I stared down at her for a few seconds, her eyes meeting mine innocently as she sat there. I studied her face for a few seconds and it suddenly hit me that she really was quite beautiful. My heart stopped for a second and I felt confused. What did I care if she was beautiful? There were many beautiful women in the world. Many beautiful women who it would be a lot less complicated to mess around with.

"I'll be sitting here, patiently waiting," she said with another smile, a wider one this time.

"Good," I said with a nod and walked out of the room, wondering why all of a sudden I felt so pleased. I walked to my room and frowned as I opened my bedroom door. There was something about Sally that was starting to get to me and I really didn't like that. Not at all.

"CHOCOLATE CHIP AND blueberry pancakes?" I laughed as Sally eagerly scarfed down her maple-syrup-covered pancakes. "I've seen everything now."

"Try some—they're delicious." She grinned at me through her bites.

"I think I'm okay. I don't need diabetes."

"Blueberries won't give you diabetes." Her eyes twinkled as she continued eating.

"No, but the chocolate and syrup will." I laughed as I dug into my spinach and feta cheese omelet. I took a bite of my whole wheat toast and watched as Sally made a face at my plate. I laughed as she licked her lips and her tongue darted out to get a drop of syrup that had run down her chin.

"Delicious," she said again, as she paused to take a sip of her coffee. I just stared at her as she drank, and then I looked around the diner we were in. There were families all around us, little kids laughing with happiness, parents struggling to stay awake, waitresses bustling around hoping to make big tips, elderly couples enjoying each other's company and the discounted meal, and while the feeling of being part of a more mainstream setting would have made me uncomfortable in most instances, at this moment I didn't mind. I was happy. I was having fun. Being with Sally was easy. I wasn't sure why I'd never really realized that before. In all our years of being friends, or rather, all the time she'd been best friends with Mila, I'd never really seen her as more than another annoying yappy girl. Though sometimes I had appreciated her beauty and sexy ass.

"So what exactly did you and Mila want to talk to me about?" I asked her as I remembered that this was meant to have been a joint breakfast—that Mila had called me yesterday, urging me to meet her and Sally for breakfast because they wanted to talk.

"It was really Mila that wanted some advice from you," Sally said with a wary smile, her eyes looking like a deer in headlights as her face went slightly red.

"Oh God, she's not having problems with TJ already, is she?" I groaned and shook my head. "I'm not sure what she wants me to do."

"I don't think she's having problems with TJ." Sally smiled and shook her head. "You'll have to ask her next time you see her."

"Yeah," I agreed. "Though it wasn't nice of her to stand you up as well. You showed up at my place pretty early."

"Yeah, she should have let me know." Sally nodded and looked down. I noticed that her tongue was licking her lips again and I wondered what they tasted like most right now: chocolate, blueberries, syrup—or a mix of all three.

"Though I suppose a free breakfast doesn't hurt."

"Free?"

"Yeah, it's on me." I winked at her. "Does that get me any rewards?"

"Rewards?" She looked at me curiously.

"Rewards, points, treats?" I grinned at her, not sure why I was flirting with her, but not wanting to stop.

"Why would you get a reward?"

"Because you want to give me one?"

"Haha, I want to give you a reward?" She glanced up at me under veiled eyelashes. "What makes you think that?"

"The way you're licking your lips and staring at the pancakes so lovingly. I think I've taken you to fantasyland." I winked at her.

"Fantasyland?" She cocked her head and laughed. "With some pancakes?"

"I think I've given you a food orgasm, at least." I stared into her eyes. "Right?"

"A food orgasm?" she said, her face turning slightly red. "Really?"

"Yeah. Though I suppose a real orgasm would have been nicer." My voice dropped as I stared at her, wanting to see how she'd react, knowing I was close to crossing a line. A line that was almost invisible.

"Uhm…" She looked away from me and I felt a knot turning in my stomach.

"Too far?" I asked her a bit too loudly, but wanting her to know I was joking, even if I was only half-joking. I was confusing even myself at this point.

"Yes, too far." She laughed, her eyes looking back up at me, a light of some emotion I didn't really recognize reflected in her irises.

"You're used to it, though. With me." I laughed and reached over. "Let me try these awesome pancakes before you scarf them all down."

"You want to try them?" She looked surprised. "After all that smack talk?"

"Hey, I'm the king of smack talk." I laughed and grabbed her fork and pressed down into the pancake and then took a large bite. It was overly sweet, though the pancake was of a good texture. The blueberries melted in my mouth along with the chocolate and I could feel an immediate sugar rush going to my head. Sally was looking at me expectantly, wondering how I was going to react to her meal. I was about to make a joke and tell her it was gross and overly sweet and a sure race to diabetes, but something stopped me. "Not bad." I chewed and swallowed and gave her a smile. "I guess I know why you're so sweet," I said and gave her another small wink.

"I told you they weren't that bad." She smiled back at me happily, her face alight and glowing as she stared at me. "Now give me my fork back. You can't finish them."

"Darn." I laughed. "I wanted to eat about ten more bites."

"Oh, Cody." She burst out laughing. "You don't even like them."

"What are you talking about?" I asked her questioningly.

"You don't like sweet stuff." She giggled. "You forget I know you well."

"I don't mind sweet stuff."

"You much prefer savory to sweet." She shook her head. "And I saw your face when you took a bite just now, you winced for a second. And then you touched your forehead as if the sugar had run there immediately."

"You noticed all that?"

"What can I say? I'm observant." She grinned. "So while I thank you for pretending you thought my choice of breakfast was delicious, I know you didn't actually think that."

"Aww, foiled again. You got me." I sat back. "So you got any plans for the rest of the day?"

"Not really." She shook her head. "You?"

"I was going to watch the game."

"The game?" She looked confused and I laughed. "Basketball?"

"Nah." I grinned at her. "It's football season."

"Oh, okay." She gave me a weak smile. "I had no clue."

"It's okay." I laughed. "Most girls don't care." I paused then. "Wait, some girls care, I know that. Don't think I'm sexist."

"I don't think you're sexist." She grinned. "I don't care if you think I'm into sports or not. We both know I'm not."

"You used to play tennis, though."

"Yeah, but I never watched it." She looked up at me then in surprise. "I can't believe you remember that. I didn't even play for very long."

"There are a lot of things I can remember about you." I grinned. "A lot of things you wouldn't want me to bring up to your future husband."

"Yeah." Her expression changed and I wondered if she was worried that I'd let out all of her secrets on her wedding day. My heart started beating erratically as I thought about Sally getting married.

"I can't believe Mila and TJ are getting married," I said, not enjoying the tightness in my chest. "We've gone and lost our best friends." I tried to laugh, though the noise sounded awkward to my own ears. "What will we do now?" I said again, trying to sound normal. I looked down at the table for a second. I wasn't sure why I was feeling out of sorts. Maybe I was more upset about TJ and Mila getting married than I'd thought initially.

CHAPTER SEVEN

Sally

"I GUESS YOU'RE going to be my new best friend, now that we've lost our best friends to each other," I said to Cody, a huge smile on my face. The smile was there to hide the fact that what I really wanted to do was pull him up and out of his seat, drag him over to me and ask him what it was that he didn't like about me. Why didn't he like me? Why didn't he love me? Why didn't he want to date me? How could he bring up things he was going to tell or not tell my future husband, while I was here hoping he would tell me *he* wanted to be my future husband?

My heart felt frozen and I knew the smile on my face was fake as hell. I'd thought the breakfast was going well. Shit, he'd been flirting with me. He'd talked about an orgasm, for heaven's sake. An orgasm! Who did that if they didn't like someone? I almost felt like he was playing with me. Testing me to see how I'd react. I wanted to shake him. I wanted to tell him he couldn't do this to me. He couldn't make me think he was interested in one breath and then push me back to the ground in the next.

"Sally and Cody, best friends forever."

I said the words like I was some little kid on the playground. I wasn't even sure where they'd come from. Was I showing all my cards too soon? Was he going to think I was some sort of weirdo? I knew as soon as the words were out of my mouth that

I'd made a mistake. A big, stupid mistake. A mistake that could cost me all the peace of mind I had left. Yet, a part of me didn't care. If I was going with this plan, I might as well just go with it and see what would happen.

"Yeah." He nodded and smiled back at me. "I guess you're my best buddy now." He slapped his hand down on top of my hand and I almost jumped at the contact. My heart started thudding erratically at the feel of his warm, strong hand on mine, and I could feel my body growing warm. "You going to be my wingwoman as well, then?" he said with another huge grin, and my stomach dropped almost immediately.

"Sure," I said, my heart both breaking and rejoicing at the same time. The feel of his hand next to mine was amazing, made me feel alive, but the pain that was striking through my entire existence at his asking me to be his wingwoman was almost excruciating. How could he be thinking of other women in this moment? Couldn't he feel our connection? How could I be the only one seeing this? Just being around him gave me energy and life, yet he didn't seem to be affected by me at all.

I blinked up at him then and I wondered to myself if I was going crazy. If I had somehow let some alien into my life. How could I be so attached and attuned to him? How could I be feeling all these emotions? So many ups and downs and he—he just seemed to be feeling nothing. It made absolutely no sense to me. Absolutely no sense at all.

PART II

Cody

NOTHINGNESS. LOVE. THE depths of the ocean. The call of the wild. The trees in the forest. The majestic evergreen of the mountain. The brown ridges creating lines that could be seen from the other side of town, hundreds of miles away. The white snowcaps teasing me, begging me to come play. Her voice softly calling to me. Death. Life. The gentle sweetness of a first kiss. The breaking of a heart. The depths of my soul. The number of times I've wanted to say sorry. Emptiness. The feeling inside my stomach as I lie in bed thinking, thinking, thinking. Wondering. Loving her more than I've ever thought was possible. Losing her to another. Desperately trying to figure out if I can reclaim her heart. Thinking, thinking, thinking.

She was mine. I was hers. We were us. And I screwed it all up.

CHAPTER EIGHT

Sally

THE MOMENT I knew Cody and I had developed a genuine deep friendship was the first night we spent together. And I don't mean *spent* as in wham-bam, thank you, ma'am, screaming orgasms and strawberries and whipped cream. Though I wouldn't have said no to any of those things—let's be honest. No, I mean, spent the night as in we were in the same bed together and I felt his body close to mine (it was heaven and hell at the same time).

It was a couple of nights ago. We'd gone out to dinner because that's what we do now, we go to dinner weekly to catch up. Don't ask! It sounds better than it is. It's great being around him, but it sucks because nothing ever happens. He doesn't try and kiss me. He doesn't try and take my hand. He doesn't try and do anything. And of course, I don't either. I mean, I've thought about it. I've dreamed about grabbing him and kissing him and sucking his tongue and putting my hands through his hair, but my nerves and fear of rejection have stopped me. Being rejected sucks, but being rejected by your new quasi-best-friend would suck even more.

But I digress; back to that night.

We'd gone out to dinner and had a few drinks and Cody asked if I wanted to go back to his place to watch a movie. Of course, I said yes. And of course, I was hoping that "watch a movie" was some sort of code word for fucking my brains out. I know, I know, I'm getting crude, but you can only be around a sexy man for so long without starting to feel like you're going to go out of your mind. But alas, alack, watching a movie meant just that.

We watched *Eternal Sunshine of the Spotless Mind*. Yes, you read that correctly. He let me choose the movie. I'm not sure why he let me pick and I'm not sure why I chose that one, but I did. A friend of mine had told me it was a good movie, so I decided, hey, why not watch it now? Not the best decision I've ever made. It's a great movie, but emotional. Full of angst and love and hate and anger and pain and soul-matey stuff that I didn't need to be watching with Cody. And of course, I started crying. I started crying for the characters and I started crying for myself. I wanted someone to love me enough to be so caught up in me that he would want to erase me from his mind to stop the pain. I mean, who wouldn't want to be loved that much? I mean, I know it's not healthy. I know my views are skewed. I know I have some issues, but don't we all?

There was this one scene where one of the characters said something like, "I'm erasing you, and I'm happy," and it made me burst into tears right away because I'd just been having thoughts about wanting to erase Cody from my mind that morning. Cody's face had looked at me in shock and I could see that I was making him uncomfortable.

"You okay?" he asked me with a worried expression. I started crying even more then because he'd been so genuine and caring. Not teasing at all, but truly worried. Truly searching in my eyes to see if I was okay.

"Yeah." I nodded and gulped. "It's just a sad movie."

"It's just a movie though, Sally." He put his arm around me

awkwardly and pulled me into his arms so that I could rest my head against his chest.

"I know," I said and closed my eyes, enjoying the feel of his chest against the side of my face. His body was so warm and comforting and it made me feel wonderful. "It's just hard to see people who are so in love fall apart from each other."

"Yeah, that's love, I suppose," Cody said softly. "Love is a temporary emotion. And so when people invest everything they have into something that is temporary, of course it will be devastating when it flees."

"You think love is temporary?" I said, my heart stilling as I listened to him. I could feel his hands rubbing my back.

"I don't think that true love is real and I don't think that any emotion lasts forever," he said simply, and I swore I felt his lips on the top of my head, though I could have been imagining it.

"I like to think there are true loves that last forever," I said, looking up at him. "That there is someone perfect made for us."

"That's why you're awesome," he said and grinned down at me. "And I'm sure that one day, you will find someone who will love you forever and ever."

"Thank you," I said, trying not to let the sadness sweep over me again. I couldn't allow him to keep dictating my moods. And I just needed to appreciate the fact that we were getting closer and we were getting to be better friends.

"Wanna watch the rest of the movie in bed?" he asked me questioningly. "No funny business, I promise, but it might be more comfortable."

"Hmm, let me think," I said with a smile, my heart racing as I gazed up at him. I could feel his palms on my waist and I could feel his body moving back and forth against mine as he breathed. This was the closest we'd been for the longest amount of time and I was enjoying it. Even if it wasn't romantic or sexual. It was close. And I was craving being close to him. In fact this was one of the best feelings I'd ever felt in my life.

"I have popcorn." He laughed. "And wine. And we can watch another movie. Or we can talk."

"Talk?" I laughed. "Talk about what?"

"Whatever you want." He made a face. "I know you girls like to talk."

"And you guys don't?" I grinned at him, wiping the tears from my eyes, feeling light all of a sudden.

"Oh, we talk, but not about the same crap you girls talk about." He grinned at me. "We talk about sports, beer, work, movies—and you girls talk about feelings and all that crap. You'd better believe TJ and I don't talk about that shit."

"But you're willing to talk about that with me? Aww, aren't I lucky?"

"Well, I want to be a good friend." He looked at me sincerely. "I'll try my best."

"Thanks, Cody," I said and then nodded. "Sure. Let's move to the bedroom, though I get to choose which side of the bed I want."

"Of course, my dear," he said and grabbed my hand as we jumped off the couch. We settled into his bed a few minutes later, laden with popcorn, potato chips, wine, beer, and some chocolate, and settled into watching the movie, sitting side-by-side and leaning back against the wall. And when the movie was done, we lay down and stared at each other and just talked and talked. We talked about everything: Kant's philosophies, our views on Israel and Palestine, his favorite football team, politics, my favorite movies. We talked about our favorite books, and at the end of the night as we both started getting sleepy and our eyes were drooping, he leaned forward and gave me a firm kiss on the lips and whispered. "You're fast becoming one of my favorite people, Sally, one of my absolute favorites." And I closed my eyes then and smiled to myself. I drifted off to sleep the happiest I'd been in months. That was when I knew that I'd wormed my way into Cody's heart in some way. Even if it wasn't exactly in the way I'd hoped for.

I'M GOING TO give you some advice. Don't play games with guys. Even if you don't think you're playing a game, think about what you're doing very carefully—very, very carefully. Guys aren't like girls. They don't analyze. They certainly don't overanalyze and they take what we say and think that's exactly what we mean. Even if the dumbest pig in Siberia would know we were being ironic or sarcastic, a man would take us at our word.

Like Cody. He took me at my word when I told him I thought we should be best friends. I knew and Mila knew and anyone with half a brain knew that I meant best friends that were also in love, but no—not Cody. He took my words literally. He really thought I wanted to be best friends and everything else that went along with that. And now, well now, here I am, surrounded by the man of my dreams day and night and hating my life. All because I decided to tell a porky pie to get closer to him. That's all I wanted. Just to spend time with him. I just wanted him to get to know me better. I wanted him to fall in love with me. I wanted him to see how perfect I was for him.

But no, that's not what happened. Sure, he thinks I'm 'awesome' and we're closer now than we've ever been, but not in the way I want. Not in the way that makes my heart thud. My heart does thud still. But generally in a sad way now. And I cry myself to sleep many nights because I realize I'm further away from him than I've ever been. Now that we're better friends, I realize that:

One, I'm not his type. Two, we don't have much in common. And three, he hasn't—as I'd secretly hoped—been harboring a secret crush on me for years. At least I don't think he has.

I could hear Cody banging around in the kitchen as I sat and waited for him to finish what he was doing. We had spent the afternoon doing a crossword puzzle together and now I was on his laptop looking up movie times. And of course, I just happened to click around and boom, up came his OkCupid account. It wasn't that I didn't know he was online dating. Of course I knew. We'd talked about dating casually and how we'd joined online dating sites and we'd laughed about all the odd people we'd seen online. That hadn't made me feel bad because that wasn't real and there had been no faces to put to mind. And no actual dates were talked about. Yes, I'd helped him write a profile, but that had made me feel closer to him because we had laughed and joked around about what he was looking for and his interests. But now that I had his profile up on the screen and I could see that he was actively on the site and messaging and talking to people, it was another story. Heat rose through my face as my stomach grumbled in emptiness. I could feel my head starting to spin as I swallowed, my heart feeling empty, the pain wallowing through me almost too much to bear as I read some of the messages on the screen. I knew I was invading his privacy and I knew I deserved the pain I was experiencing for being so nosey, but I just couldn't stop myself.

"You nearly ready, Sally?" Cody's voice was warm as he stood in the doorway looking at me. "I told TJ and Mila we'd be there at seven and I still have to pick some other friends up."

"Yeah, gimme a minute." I gave him a weak smile and looked back at the computer screen. Cody had left open his OkCupid dating account on the screen and I could see all the women he'd been exchanging messages with. I scrolled through the page to see what they looked like, unable to stop myself, even though I knew I shouldn't. I then clicked to see the girls he'd liked. My stomach dropped as I stared at all their beautiful faces. They all looked the same: long, dark, straight hair, big blue eyes, fine beautiful features, all were skinny and all had that "I'm cool, look at me" look on their faces. I could feel embarrassment sweeping through me as it hit me, maybe for the first time, that I was just not Cody's type. Not at all. Nothing about me fit what he was looking for in a woman. I wasn't sure how I'd missed that fact. I knew I shouldn't read the messages, but I couldn't stop myself.

"What movies are showing?"

"What?" I blinked up at him.

"Aren't you looking up movie times?" He walked toward me and my heart stopped as I clicked on a new tab and typed in "movie times" quickly into Google.

"Yeah, yeah, sorry, I put in the wrong zip code." I said lamely. "Let me check the right one now."

"Okay." He nodded. "Let me go and call TJ and tell them we're running late."

"Sure, and sorry about the delay. My head has been all over the place lately."

"Hey, no worries, Sally." He gave me a huge smile and my heart melted, even though I was in a really low place. "We'll get there."

"Yeah, we will."

"And you know I'm here to talk if you ever need someone, right?"

"Yeah, I know." I nodded. "Thanks." I watched as he headed out of the room and I tried not to cry. This whole situation was a lot harder than I'd thought it was going to be. I was getting to know Cody on a deeper level and I was falling for him harder and harder. Only, he wasn't falling for me. Yes, he was growing closer to me. Yes, I knew he saw me in a different light now, but I also knew that wasn't a romantic light. I just wanted him to pull me closer to him. I wanted him to kiss me, to touch me, to want me, yet he seemed to have no interest in growing closer to me in that way—and that killed me. And I knew that if it didn't kill me, it would just leave me empty and alone. I wanted to slap myself. I needed to get some self-respect. I needed to grow some self-esteem. I needed to love myself enough to accept that he just didn't want me that way, and I needed to move on with my life. Or at least stop whining to myself. I was getting fed up with my own tears and heartache. I just needed to get over it already.

"HOW DID WE end up choosing a horror movie?" I whispered to Mila as we walked into the movie theater ahead of the guys. "You know I hate horror movies. I'm going to scream and embarrass myself."

"You won't." She gave me a sly grin and my eyes narrowed.

"You chose the movie, didn't you?" I growled under my breath. "Mila, how could you do this to me? You know I wanted to see a rom-com or something."

"The guys don't wanna watch a rom-com. Plus, if we do a horror, whenever you feel scared you can grab ahold of Cody and he can protect you."

"Mila," I groaned. "That's not about to happen."

"You never know." She shrugged and smiled. "You need to up the stakes."

"I don't want to up the stakes." I sighed. "This is too much already."

"What are you two whispering about?" Cody came up from behind me and nearly made me jump.

"Nothing," I said quickly and then paused. What if he'd heard some of what I had said? "Well, I was just complaining that Mila chose a horror movie and she knows I hate them."

"I'm here to protect you if you feel scared." He grinned at me and my heart fluttered. "Just sit next to me."

"Aww, thanks, Cody," I said, my heart racing. Maybe he really was coming around?

"No worries, that's what friends are for." He grinned at me and overtook Mila and me and walked into our theater. "Let's try and get some seats towards the top. I hate being too close to the screen."

"Sure," I mumbled as I gave Mila a small glare, my stomach sinking at his use of the word 'friends'.

"It'll be fine," she mumbled, smiling, and then reached behind to grab TJ's hand. "Honey, will you protect me as well, if I get scared?"

"I'll protect you any day of the week. Any second of the day." TJ pulled her to him and kissed her cheek. "I'll protect you from the grave."

"Aww, my love." Mila beamed and I tried not to groan in envy. Why did they have to be so sickeningly sweet all the time? I could still remember when they used to trade barbs back and forth. I could still remember when Mila was in my position, loving a man she thought didn't even want to give her the time of day. Only life had looked favorably upon her. Life had given her the love of the man she wanted. I wasn't so lucky.

I wanted to slap myself for my thoughts. I knew I was feeling sorry for myself. I knew I was part of—if not all of—the reason I was feeling miserable, and that envy was a horrible trait. I knew it, but I just couldn't stop myself from dwelling on my despair and heartache. I needed to make a change. I needed to get over it. I'd been reading online articles about unrequited love and for all intents and purposes, it seemed like I just needed to cut Cody out of my life and move on, though I felt loathe to do that. Instead, I was holding on to some inner hope, some flame of fire inside me that wouldn't die out. I was wasting my life away and slowly eroding my soul from the inside. If he was my soul mate and I was his soul, then I knew we were both destined for a fiery fate.

"Come on, Sally," Cody called me from a couple of steps up, and I hurried up my pace to catch up with him. "You were spacing out again?"

"No." I shook my head.

"Are you really that scared of horror movies?" His eyes searched my face. "If you want, we can watch something else. If you're really that scared."

"No, I'm fine, but thank you."

"No worries." He smiled and grabbed my hand and squeezed. "I'm sure the witches won't come and get you. Or the bogeyman."

"Yay for that." I rolled my eyes at him and giggled. "Hopefully they don't come and attack me in my bed tonight."

"I can protect you there as well." He raised an eyebrow at me and then winked.

"Oh, really?" I gazed at him and winked back. "How do you propose to do that?"

"Well, I think my presence alone would scare them off, but I'd put my arms around you and hold you close and then I'd…" His voice trailed off as Mila and TJ sat down next to us. "Wow, you two slow-coaches decided to join us."

"Why, of course." Mila gave her brother a look. "Did you miss us?"

"Do I miss heartburn?" Cody retorted, and I giggled. He looked up at me and smiled. "Aren't you glad you have me now, and not just Mila?"

"Oh, so glad."

"Why would she be glad to have you?" Mila gave him a look.

"I can do things for her that you can't," he said softly and my heart fluttered, but this time not in a romantic way.

"What things can you do for her that I can't?" Mila asked with a scoff.

"You mean, aside from impregnating her?" Cody said with a laugh and my face grew hot.

"Cody!" Mila looked shocked. "You're disgusting."

"I'm disgusting? You asked the question." His face went all innocent. "And unless I've been lied to all my life about your gender, I don't think you can knock Sally up."

"I just can't with you, Cody Brookstone." Mila rolled her eyes and looked at me. I knew the look was saying, *I have no idea why you like this Neanderthal,* and I grinned back at her. I had no idea why I was so in love with Cody. Maybe I secretly loved his very immature side. I wasn't sure what it was, but I knew he always made me laugh.

"You just can't with me, Mila Brookstone, soon to be Walker," Cody said and moved his head back and forth. "You just can't do what with me, sister?" He snapped his fingers in a sorority girl movement and we all started laughing.

"TJ, I have no idea how you remained best friends with Cody for all these years." Mila looked at her fiancé. "It seems to me that you are suspect yourself, for being his best friend."

"What if I told you I only stayed friends with him to be close to you?" TJ said dryly, and Cody groaned out loud.

"Dude, why are you feeding her this bullshit?" Cody shook his head.

"You don't know it's bullshit," Mila said and then laughed. "Though even I think that was a bullshit line, TJ Walker."

"Hey, hey, don't attack me now." He put his hands up and laughed. "Help me, Sally."

"How can I help you?" I grinned back at him.

"Can you guys be quiet, please?" A portly guy sitting in front of us turned around and glared at us. "The movie is going to start soon and I don't need to be listening to your commentary."

"Yes, sir." Cody saluted him and we all laughed. The guy gave us one last glare and a huff and turned back around. I looked over at Cody, who winked at me again, and I giggled as we all sat there in silence. I felt Cody reach over and rub my leg and I looked up at him in surprise. He gave me a small wink and I slapped his hand away. He then grabbed my hand and I looked at him in confusion.

"Thumb war?" he mouthed and I nodded with a smile.

"One, two, three, four, I declare a thumb war," I said quietly as our thumbs tackled each other's as if we were still little kids. I tried my hardest to hold his thumb down, but not because I wanted to win. I tried my hardest because I didn't want the game to end and for me to lose the contact of his hand, which was so warm and silky that it was making me feel things in places I hadn't felt things in a while.

"THAT MOVIE SUCKED," Cody said as we left the movie theater. "I need a beer to get over how much it sucked."

"I agree, it wasn't that scary." I laughed as I walked by his side. "I wouldn't mind getting a cocktail to get over my lack of fear."

"Hey, guys, as much as we'd love to join you for a drink, TJ and I have plans early in the morning, so I'm not sure that that will be possible." Mila made a face. "Have a drink on me, though."

"You're not coming?" I looked at her in disappointment, my heart racing. As much as I wanted to spend time alone with Cody, and we had plenty of times already, it felt weird to be going to a bar, just the two of us. It almost felt like a date. Though I knew it wasn't. At all.

"Sadly, no." Mila shook her head and her eyes stared into mine with a glint. My heart started racing as I realized she was doing this on purpose. She was trying to get me to make a move. A real move. I knew it was time to just see if it was ever going to go anywhere, but the whole moment was just scaring the shit out of me.

"Where shall we go, Sally?" Cody looked at me with a questioning look. "You're not going to flake out on me as well, are you?"

"Would I do that?" I laughed, my heart fluttering. He wanted me to come? I tried to tell myself he didn't really care if I came or not. I tried to tell myself all he wanted to do was grab a drink and he didn't care who was coming with him, but it was hard to tell myself that when all the hope in me was praying to God that it was because he secretly had feelings for me and wanted to spend the evening with me.

"I hope not." He gave me a winning smile and then turned to Mila and TJ. "Okay, well, it was good seeing you guys. I'll get Sally home safely."

"You'd better." Mila pointed her finger at him and then she looked over at me. "You sure you want to go out with Cody?"

"Sure, it'll be fun." I nodded and she winked at me and I tried not to laugh in giddiness.

"Ready, Sally?" Cody grabbed ahold of my hand and pulled me away from Mila and TJ. "Let's leave these two lovebirds to figure something out. And let's go and get a drink. Bye, guys."

"Bye, guys," I repeated to Mila and TJ as I gave them a small wave goodbye, wondering what I was getting myself into.

"YOU WANT A glass of wine?" Cody asked me as we walked into a crowded bar.

"I think I'll have a cocktail, actually." I laughed. "A cosmo, thanks."

"Okay." He nodded. "Wait here for me and I'll be back." He looked toward the packed crowd in front of him. "Unless you'd like to join the meat market with me?"

"No, I'm good here, thanks." I smiled and readjusted my bag strap on my shoulder. "You go ahead and get the drinks. I'm thirsty."

"Anything to oblige you, my dear." He grinned and continued on his way to the bar. I stood there watching him for a few seconds and then looked around me to check out the scene. There was a good mix of people, ranging from mid-twenties to mid-forties, and there seemed to be a lot of singles flirting with each other. I watched two girls who were checking out a particularly good-looking blond guy and trying to make eye contact with him, but he didn't seem to notice them at all. I grinned to myself as I watched one of the girls flick her hair and stare him down, but still he didn't look at her. And then, because this is how life always goes, the hot guy looked up and stared at me. And because I'm awkward in these situations, I just continued to stare at him with the grin on my face. When I realized we were making eye contact, I looked away quickly and I could feel myself blushing.

"Hi, there." I heard a deep voice right next to me and I looked up and saw the hot blond guy, who was even better-looking closer up than he had been from a distance. His hair was a deep gold and his eyes were big, bright, and a piercing blue.

His face held a golden tan and his pearly white teeth were perfectly even as he smiled at me.

"Hi," I said with a small smile. I looked over his shoulder and saw the two girls glaring at me.

"Waiting on a friend?" he said, looking around him before he looked back at me.

"Kinda." I nodded. "You?"

"I just came for a drink. By myself." He smiled again. "It's been a long week."

"Work?" I asked him.

"Yeah." He nodded and fake shuddered. "I'm an attorney and I've been in the middle of the most tedious document reviews for the last two weeks."

"Sounds painful."

"It was. My night is looking up now, though," he said, his eyes twinkling as he looked at me. "Would you like a drink?"

"Oh, my friend went to get me a drink," I said and looked toward the bar to see if I could see Cody. I felt weird saying he was my friend, but what else could I say? 'The man I love who doesn't care about me'? No way.

"Oh, okay." He nodded and his expression became thoughtful. "My name is Tom, by the way."

"Nice to meet you, Tom. I'm Sally."

"Sally," he said with a grin and then held his hand out.

"Something amusing about my name?" I asked curiously as I shook his hand.

"My sister's favorite doll when she was growing up was called Sally," he said with a smile.

"Oh."

"I have fond memories of the name." He laughed. "She used to make me play house and I was Sally's favorite uncle."

"Well, that's good, then." I laughed. "I can't say I have any similar stories about Toms, though I loved watching the Tom Sawyer movie when I was younger."

"Aww, I haven't seen it. I'll have to check it out," he said and then he took a step closer to me. "So, what do you say about getting out of here?"

"Getting out of here?" I swallowed quickly. Tom had gone from zero to a hundred in less than ten seconds.

"Yeah, maybe we could go grab a bite and talk?" He leaned over and whispered in my ear. "And maybe we could have some play time." I felt his hand on the small of my back and I froze. Damn! He was smooth and I had totally not expected the immediate come-on. He'd seemed so sweet and nice in the two minutes we'd been talking.

"Uhm, I, uhm…" I stuttered, not knowing what to say as I felt him tapping my ass. "Hey," I said as I jumped slightly.

"Sorry, I couldn't resist." He grinned. "You have a nice ass."

"Uh, thanks," I said, suddenly feeling uncomfortable.

"So, what do you say to maybe going back to my place?" he said with a wink and a quick lick of his lips.

"Hey, what's going on here?" Cody arrived back then with our drinks and I could have thrown my arms around him.

"Can I help you?" Tom looked over at Cody with a frown.

"I'm wondering if I can help you?" Cody's face was unreadable as he stood there. "Sally, are you okay?"

"I'm fine." I nodded, not really sure what to say.

"Oh, this is your friend?" Tom looked at Cody and then back at me. "If he's looking for a gay bar, this isn't the place, but maybe when we head to my place, we can drop him off at 'Out of the Closet.' It's a hot spot for men."

"Excuse me?" Cody's voice was deep and I knew he was pissed.

"Oh, sorry, you're not gay?" Tom said with a shrug and I felt his hand on my back again. "Want to dance before we leave?"

"Leave?" Cody's voice was louder and angrier as he stared now directly at me. "What's going on, Sally?"

"Uhm, nothing," I squeaked out, not really knowing what to say. "We just met," I explained lamely.

"I saw her beauty from across the room and had to come and say hello," Tom said, licking his lips again. "Especially when I saw the grin she was giving me. Your lips are beautiful," he said as he stared at me. "So full and juicy, oooohhhmm." He winked at me.

My face grew bright red as I stood there.

"I think you need to leave." Cody looked at Tom. "Like, now."

"What?" Tom blinked at him. "What are you talking about?"

"Sally and I are here together on a date. You need to leave."

"She told me she was here with her friend," Tom said, looking annoyed. "Seems like she isn't considering this a date, dude."

"You've got thirty seconds to move before things get nasty," Cody said, his voice low. "And just so you know, I punch very much like a man with over two hundred pounds behind him."

"Do you want me to leave?" Tom looked at me and I could see his eyes on my lips and then on my breasts. All of a sudden, his good looks weren't so enamoring.

"Yeah, I think that's best," I said softly as I stepped away from him.

"Cock tease," he said with a shake of his head as he looked at me and then walked away. I stood there wanting to go after him and slap him across the face, but instead I just stood there and stared at Cody, not really knowing what to say. Not really knowing what had just gone on between us.

"That guy was a douche," Cody said as he handed me my cosmo.

"He seemed okay, at first," I said and took a quick sip. "He was very handsome."

"I didn't realize you'd come out to pick someone up," he snapped. "I didn't realize you were using me."

"I didn't come out to pick someone up," I said with a slight attitude.

"What were you telling him before I got here that made him think you guys were going to be hooking up?"

"I didn't tell him anything." I shook my head and pursed my lips. Why was he getting upset with me?

"Did you fancy him?" Cody looked at me suspiciously. "He was a good-looking guy."

"I mean, yeah, he was cute." I shrugged. "What does it matter?"

"It doesn't matter." Cody pursed his lips. "I'm just trying to figure out if you want me to go and get him back here so you can leave with him."

"I don't want to leave with him." I sighed. "He came over to me. We barely spoke for a few minutes."

"You didn't seem to be turning him away." Cody chugged at his beer as he stared at me.

"I didn't turn him away because he had just come up to me."

"I saw he had his hands on your back." Cody's eyes never left my face as he continued chugging his beer.

"He had his hands on my ass, too," I snapped, feeling annoyed.

"And you liked that?" Cody looked pissed and he slammed his empty beer bottle down on a table next to us.

"No, I didn't like that." I shook my head and sipped some more of my drink.

"Finish your drink," Cody said aggressively as he came closer to me.

"What?" I frowned up at him, not sure why he was acting so funky.

"Finish your drink," he said again, staring down at me with alert eyes. "Then we'll dance."

"Dance?" I said, surprised. "You want to dance?"

"We'll dance and then we'll leave." He shrugged.

"Leave and go where?"

"We'll see." He continued to watch my face. "Wherever we want."

"I guess." I sipped my drink quicker this time. My heart was racing and I wasn't sure what was going on. As soon as I finished my drink, Cody took the glass out of my hand and placed it on the table next to me.

"Come," he said as he grabbed my hand and pulled me toward the dance floor. "Let's dance."

"Okay," I said, following behind him quickly. He pushed us through the throngs of people and then stopped and pulled me into his arms and started moving back and forth. "This isn't a slow song," I said as I moved with him as best as I could in time to the music.

"So?" He grinned, holding me close to him. I could feel his warm body pressed up against mine closely and it felt like heaven. I decided to just go with it and I closed my eyes and rested my head on his shoulder as we moved. Something felt different between us and I wasn't sure what it was. I didn't want to think about it. I didn't want to overanalyze. Part of me wondered if he'd been jealous of Tom, but then I didn't want to think that too strongly. I didn't want to hope that maybe he did have feelings for me after all. That could only lead to more heartache. But as he held me in his arms and we moved back and forth with our bodies pressed together, I couldn't stop the feeling of hope and excitement spreading through me.

"LET'S GO TO my place," Cody said as we left the bar a few hours and five drinks later. We were both buzzed to a point of almost being drunk and we'd been holding hands all night.

"Are you sure?" I said, my words nearly slurring as I looked up at his handsome face.

"Yes." He nodded and then it happened. The moment I'd been awaiting for what seemed like most of my life.

Cody pulled me into his arms, leaned his head down, and I felt his lips pressing down on mine, softly at first and then with more pressure. I felt his hands in my hair, pulling my tresses, as he deepened the kiss and I felt my knees trembling as his tongue pried its way into my mouth. He tasted of beer and apples and I kissed him back passionately, my tongue entering his mouth smoothly. Immediately, he began to suck on my tongue and I felt him pushing his body closer to mine. I reached my hands up around his neck and played with his hair, reaching into his scalp and taking in his entire essence. I writhed against him as I felt his right hand sliding against my side and then reaching towards my breast. I moaned as his fingers rubbed against me and we both pulled back slightly, breathing deeply.

"Let's get out of here," he said, his voice deep and husky.

"Okay." I nodded, not knowing if I was in a dream or not and not even caring.

"My place?"

"Sure." I nodded, knowing what he was asking and not even sure how we'd gotten to this place. I could feel my entire body shaking in sweet anticipation and the hope in me that had been starting to fade erupted into huge flames once again, and I thought to myself that my moment had finally come.

CHAPTER NINE

Cody

SALLY'S HANDS WERE on my naked back and her nails were digging sharply into my skin, just like I liked it. Her body felt warm against mine and I ran my hands down to her stomach eagerly and played around in her belly button. I knew that was an erogenous zone and Sally's writhing against me let me know that I hadn't lost my touch. I kissed her lips softly and then moved my tongue down her silky neck and to her collarbone. Her black bra-straps interrupted my movement and my hands automatically moved up to bring them down, but I stopped myself. As much as I wanted her braless, I didn't want to rush it. Our clothes had come off pretty quickly, but we still had on our underwear. I felt extremely hard in my briefs and I knew she could feel my erection next to her. She was wearing a lacey black bra and panties and it took everything I could do to not rip them off of her.

"Oh, Cody." She moaned as my hand moved to the top of her panties and she stilled on my bed.

"Yes, Sally." I groaned as my fingers slipped inside her panties and then withdrew quickly as she gasped out loud. I wanted to touch all of her. I wanted to feel her wetness. I wanted to slip my fingers inside of her and bring her to orgasm before I fucked her hard.

"Cody," she moaned as she ran her fingers down my chest and over my boxer shorts. She wasn't as hesitant as I was and I felt her squeezing my hardness between her fingers before she slipped her hands into my boxers and ran her fingers up and down, squeezing the tip gently. I groaned as her fingers worked their magic on me and before I knew it I was taking my briefs off and throwing them to the floor. I looked up into Sally's eyes and they were full of lust and pleasure. I couldn't stop myself anymore and I found myself unhooking the back of her bra and peeling it off. I stared at her beautiful breasts for a few seconds before lowering my mouth to her right nipple and sucking on it. She moaned loudly as she continued to pleasure me with her hands and I found my teeth tugging and pulling on her nipple as my fingers played with her other breast. I then found myself kissing down her stomach toward her panties. I wanted to make her come. I wanted to hear her screaming my name.

I felt her body stilling as I reached her panties and I grinned to myself. My teeth grabbed the top of her panties and I pulled them down slowly, enjoying her scent as I worked my way down her legs. Once her panties were off, I kissed back up her legs and parted her thighs. I looked up at her face, and her mouth was slightly parted as she waited for me to continue. I leaned down and placed my face in her wetness, my tongue working its magic on her as she trembled beneath me. I felt heady with power as I brought her to the brink of orgasm and I could feel her hands in my hair as she shook beneath me. I knew she was close to orgasm and so I paused and kissed my way back up to her lips before lowering myself onto her. I positioned my hardness between her legs and just rubbed it there as I kissed her. She groaned as her arms went around my back, and she spread her legs wider, wanting that release, needing me to enter her as bad as I wanted to enter her. She was wet against my hardness and I positioned myself at her entrance, ready to bring us both the release we both craved and needed. Her breasts were crushed against my chest and I kissed her hard, my tongue devouring her mouth as her fingers squeezed my butt-cheeks.

I slipped the tip of my cock inside of her and then looked down at her face. My whole body was on fire and all I craved was bringing her to orgasm. I wanted to hear her screaming my name. I wanted to fuck her slowly and then quickly. I wanted to flip her over and take her from the back. I wanted her on her knees, sucking me off and then begging me to fuck her again.

It was then that I froze. I could feel her legs squeezing together, forcing me farther inside of her, and as much as I wanted to take her, I knew it was a mistake. Not like this. Not with Sally. I couldn't just fuck her and expect to go on like normal the next day. And I knew she was drunk. And I was drunk. And I knew she might regret it. She might resent me. Hate me, even. She might think I was taking advantage of her. Or she might make it more complicated than it had to be. I rolled over and lay next to her on the bed and she looked at me in confusion.

"What's going on?" she purred, her eyes hazy as she gazed at me.

"I think we're making a mistake," I said, too harshly, my eyes on her heaving breasts, my hand on her stomach.

"Huh?" She looked confused and I felt her hand reaching down to touch my hardness again. I groaned as her fingers worked their magic. I knew that if she continued, I was going to blow, and I wasn't sure how I felt about that.

"I just don't think..." I paused as her fingers tightened their grip. "Sally." I groaned and closed my eyes as my body shuddered. My fingers worked their way down to her wetness and I ran them across her quivering bud. I felt her whole body trembling as I played with her. "Sally," I said again as I slipped a finger inside of her. I felt her contract as I slid another finger inside. "We can't do this."

"Why?" she said sexily as her fingers left my cock and reached down on top of my hand. "We can."

"Sally." I felt her fingers pushing my hand down harder, so that my fingers were going deeper inside of her.

"I want to feel you inside of me." She moaned as she guided my hand faster. I grew harder at her actions, knowing just how bad she wanted me.

"I want to be inside of you," I muttered under my breath, but I withdrew my fingers from her and turned to face her. "I don't want us to ruin our friendship," I said, feeling like a fraud as I looked at the hurt on her face. "I don't want this to complicate anything."

"What?" She blinked up at me.

"I just don't think this is the right thing for us to do," I said again, my hardness and everything in me disagreeing with the words coming out of my mouth. "I don't want to lose what we have. Our friendship means the world to me."

"I see," she said, and I watched as she pulled the sheet up over her naked body.

"Do you?" I said, looking at her, already regretting my decision.

"Sure." She nodded and then yawned widely. "I'm drunk and tired, so I should probably just go to sleep now."

"Sally, I..." I started and paused as she closed her eyes. "Okay," I said finally and lay back next to her. I so badly wanted to pull her on top of me and let her ride me until the sun came up, but I knew that I had to go with my gut and my gut was telling me that if we had sex, everything would change, and I wasn't sure I could deal with the expectations she might have of me, if that were to happen.

CHAPTER TEN

Sally

"SO, WHAT DO you want to do tonight?" Mila asked me eagerly, her eyes alert as she gazed at me. I knew she was concerned about my wellbeing after my not-quite-hookup with Cody. She had been calling me for the last couple of days and had finally convinced me to meet up with her. I hadn't wanted to, but she'd said she'd send the police over to my house for a wellness check if I didn't.

"Tonight?" I responded slowly. I didn't want to do anything but go home and sleep in my bed.

"Yeah, tonight, as in a few hours from now." Mila rolled her eyes at me. "You know, what they call the time when the sun goes down."

"I didn't know you wanted to do anything tonight," I continued slowly again. "Don't you and TJ have plans?"

"No, we don't have plans. That's why I'm asking you what you want to do. In fact, I told TJ I didn't want to go to the movies with him because I wanted to hang out with you."

"Why did you do that?" I said softly, wanting to scream and shout *I don't want to hang out tonight. I just want to cry away my sorrows at the fact that Cody doesn't love me. And didn't even find me sexy enough to make love to me.* That part still stung the most, especially considering how close we'd come. My body was still tingling, thinking about him and his moves. A part of me wished I had just pushed him down on the bed and sat on him and taken everything into my own hands, but that would have made everything even more awkward.

"Because I'm not going to let you go home and cry away your sorrows." Mila gave me a look. "Or think about what an idiot Cody is for not just sealing the deal." She rolled her eyes and shook her head.

"What?" My face turned red as I looked at her, dumbfounded. "Can you read my mind?"

"No, of course I can't read your mind." She laughed. "But I have been where you are." She made a face. "I know Cody hurt your feelings."

"I don't care about Cody." I made a face back at her and then grimaced. "Okay, obviously that's a lie, but what can I say?"

"That he's a dumb fool."

"I just don't understand," I whined. "We were this close to having sex. I thought we were both into it. He was practically inside of me." I made a face at her. "Sorry for TMI."

"Haha, can we ever have TMI?" She grinned. "But yeah, he's an idiot and he probably ended up with blue balls."

"Shit, I ended up with blue balls." I groaned. "I'm just so embarrassed."

"Don't be embarrassed."

"I'm embarrassed and hurt." My voice lowered. "Am I that grotesque and ugly?"

"Of course not." Mila frowned at me. "You know that, right?"

"I know nothing." I shook my head. "And then for him to randomly text me yesterday and tell me he was going on a date. Like, how could he? Is he trying to stab me in the back?"

"I think he's just trying to make sure everything is cool with you guys." Mila sighed. "He is a guy, and he seems to be a bigger idiot than most of them."

"Yeah, I guess he wanted to let me know 'Hey, the other night meant nothing and I'm moving on to bigger and better.' He's going to end up with some hottie who he does want to sleep with and marry. Unlike me, who turned him off."

"It's just a date, Sally. It doesn't mean anything." Mila touched my arm. "He's not moving on to anything. He probably didn't even realize how hurtful he was being. I'm sure his text meant nothing. The date means nothing. Trust me."

"It means a lot." I gave a big sigh. "Did you see her photos? And did you hear how he talked about her and how much he showed us of her profile? He's really into her. Like he thinks she's his perfect mate or something. I've never received so many texts and screenshots from him in my life."

"He's a guy and he's just into the fact that she takes dance classes. He's probably hoping she's a stripper or something." Mila made a face.

"That doesn't make me feel better." I groaned.

"Yeah, but let's be real, she's probably a ballet dancer or tap or something lame." She offered up an awkward smile.

"So that means she's flexible." I made a face. "Still not making me feel better."

"Oh, Sally. You really don't know who she is. What if her photos are like five years old—or even worse, ten years old?"

"I bet they're not." I looked into her wide brown eyes. "But thanks for trying to make me feel better."

"It's just a first date. Not like they're getting married."

"Yeah, but he's going on first dates and telling me about them. A few days after we nearly had sex." I looked down to try and stop the tears from coming. "That means he couldn't care less about me."

"No, it means he trusts you enough to tell you about his dates," Mila said softly.

"I don't think that means much." I half-laughed as I looked back up. "I don't think Cody is shy about talking about going on dates."

"Yeah, but he also asked your advice on where he should take her and what he should wear and if he should take her a first-date present."

"Mila…" I looked at her with narrowed eyes. "Do you think that's some sort of consolation prize? Me telling him where I think he should take her? Honestly, I wanted to rip my heart out and throw it on the floor when he started asking me what I thought."

"Oh, Sally, you're so melodramatic." Mila looked at me in concern. "We need to make lemonade out of lemons."

"It's a little hard when we have limes." I glared at her. "Actually, scratch that, we don't even have limes, we have grapefruit. Big, stinky, sour grapefruit. No amount of sugar can make them as sweet as lemonade."

"Oh, Sally." Mila giggled.

"My misery is making you laugh?" I gave her a quick smile. "Really?"

"I'm sorry, I suck as a friend." She giggled some more and I couldn't stop myself from joining in.

"It's fine. I am being melodramatic. It's not like they're getting married." I paused. "But if that fool comes to me and asks me how he should propose, I will kill him."

"Nope." Mila shook her head. "If he's dumb enough to do something like that, I will kill him for you."

"We can kill him together." I winked at her and she burst out laughing.

"Sounds like a plan." She paused. "So what's the plan for

tonight?

"You still want to go out?"

"I'm not letting you go home by yourself to just think about Cody on his date."

"Why not? It sounds like a delightfully dreadful night." I bit down on my lower lip. "I can imagine what they're eating. If they're holding hands. If he gives her a good-night kiss. Wait, she might be forward, so maybe she'll go for the good-night kiss. Maybe she'll invite him up for a nightcap. Then maybe he'll go. And one thing will lead to another, and next thing you know, it's nine months later and there's a baby Cody and I'm asked to be the godmother. And then I can just kill myself."

"Oh, Sally." Mila looked like she wanted to start laughing again. "I thought *I* had an overactive imagination."

"Is it imagination if it's likely to be true? Especially if he still has blue balls."

"Shall we go to a club?" Mila suggested, trying to change the subject. "We can dance and maybe flirt it up with some hotties."

"What would TJ think of that?"

"He wouldn't care." She shrugged. "Plus, this is for you."

"I don't know about going to a club. I wouldn't mind dancing, but I do not want to go home and get dressed up. I'm not in a sexy or slutty mood." I made a face. "And I don't feel like shaving my legs." I laughed at the expression on Mila's face. "Hey, it's been a few days."

"No judgment here." She laughed. "I haven't shaved above the knee this week."

"TJ doesn't mind?"

"TJ knows better than to say anything." She laughed. "I'm getting a Brazilian for him next week. He can deal with some hair for a couple of days."

"Ooh, you getting a landing strip?"

"Dunno." She shook her head. "But most probably."

"Lucky," I said wistfully.

"Lucky?" She looked at me like I was crazy. "How is that lucky? Waxing down there is pain I could do without."

"I wish I had someone to wax down there for."

"You could do it for yourself," she suggested.

"Are you crazy?" I laughed. "I love myself enough to not put myself through that pain for nothing."

"Oh, Sally." She laughed. "What am I going to do with you?"

"Find me a Prince Charming—anyone who can get my sorry mind off of Cody."

"So what about we go to a bar, then? We don't have to get sexied-up, but we can look good." She grinned.

"I guess I can do a bar." I nodded. "I can get drunk off of my ass and then dance on the bar top."

"You're going to dance on the bar top *Coyote Ugly* style?"

"If you get me drunk enough." I winked at her.

"Oh, I'll get you drunk enough." She grinned. "This I have to see."

"You just want me to embarrass myself." I laughed.

"No, I just want you to have fun." She grinned back at me. "And maybe if we get drunk enough, we can both do it."

"Yeah, that would be cool." I grinned back at her. "And if TJ ever finds out, he will ban us from being friends."

"TJ can't ban me from anything." She laughed. "Well, I guess it depends what he's trying to ban me from and what he's offering me in return, but he can't just *ban me* ban me."

"Uh huh, does TJ know that?"

"No." She giggled. "He can think whatever he wants to think. And if he thinks he can ban me from something, then let him think that."

"Cody can ban me from anything he wants to." I closed my eyes. "Whatever he wants, I'd do. Whatever he said, I'd listen to. Just for the chance to be with him. Damn, if I had another chance at a night with him, I'd do whatever he wanted me to do in the bedroom."

"Sally…" Mila's voice sounded exasperated.

"I know, I sound pathetic." I opened my eyes and looked at her. "This is what your brother has done to me." I put my hands up in the air and then clutched my heart. "Oh, broken heart of mine, how will I ever live and love another again? Cody Brookstone has stolen you away from me and I fear you may never be mine again." I shook my head melodramatically and fell back into the chair behind me. Mila just stood there, watching me with a semi-concerned expression, and I knew she was wondering if she'd made a mistake by bringing up her plan in the first place. It wasn't working out well. If anything, the added friendship Cody and I now had was threatening to tear me in two. I didn't want to be his confidante and best friend. I wanted to be his lover and the love of his life.

"This is the bar all the hot guys go to?" I looked at Mila with a discouraged face as we walked into Random's, the bar Mila had been building up for the last hour.

"Yes." She gave me a weak smile and I watched her face turn toward the bar and the two middle-aged balding men who were sitting there drinking beers. "Maybe we're early."

"It's nine thirty." I gave her a look. "When do the hotties come out?"

"I don't know." She shrugged. "Ten thirty?"

"Uh, okay." I sighed, my spirit sinking. "Exactly who told you this was the happening place for single women?"

"Yelp," Mila admitted sheepishly.

"Yelp!" I groaned. "You know the bar owner probably posted some fake reviews to attract suckers like us." I shook my head and looked around the bar once again. "And it looks like it only worked on us." Except for us and the two middle-aged men at the bar, there was a big bulky tattooed guy sitting with a really skinny girl who looked like she was high on drugs. The bar was dark, dirty, and dingy, and I was confident that I would be spending no time dancing on the bar top this evening, or any other evening here.

"Let's just get one drink and we can go somewhere else," Mila said encouragingly as she walked toward the bar. "Maybe the first drink will make us feel better."

"Of course alcohol will make us feel better. The question is do we want to feel better in this dump?"

"Sally." Mila looked at me with widened eyes as we both realized that the bartender had heard me.

"You ladies want a drink?" He looked over at me and barely bat an eyelid.

"Sure," I said and reached into my purse to grab some money, feeling slightly embarrassed that he'd heard me. What if he turned out to be the bar owner? It wasn't his fault that he ran a dumpy bar. I mean, he was trying to gain new clientele it seemed, if his fake Yelp reviews were to be believed.

"What do you want?" he said again, looking bored. The expression on his face almost made me turn back around.

"We'll get two vodka sprites, please," Mila said. "Ketel One, if you have it."

"Ketel what?" the bartender asked, looking confused.

"Ketel One Vodka?" Mila said hesitantly. "It's, uhm, a brand."

"I have Smirnoff."

"That's fine," she said quickly, and I sighed. "This is going to be a long night," I whispered to her. "I might have been happier lying in bed, crying my eyes out."

"Sally, that's not funny," Mila chided me, but I could see the smile in her eyes. "I promise the next bar will be much better."

"Uh huh, don't make promises you can't keep."

"I keep my promises." She looked hurt.

"You said this place would be swarming with hotties and the only thing I think it's swarming with is Hep B and C."

"Sally," she chided me again, but this time we both started laughing. The bartender handed us our drinks and we slid onto the two bar stools in front of us. I saw the two middle-aged men giving us the once-over and I gave one of them a scornful look. As if! To my shock, the guy stuck his tongue out of his mouth and flicked it against his lips. I looked away from him quickly and then at Mila.

"I am going to kill you," I mouthed to her before taking a huge gulp of my drink. "And it will be a painful death. A very, very painful death."

"Sorry." She grinned and downed her drink. "Not too painful, I hope."

"As painful as Cody was the other night with his blue balls," I said with a straight face and then we both started laughing. I wasn't sure why I found it so funny. I still felt humiliated and rejected, but Mila had been right. It was better for me to be out of the house, where I didn't have to spend my time feeling sorry for myself and crying over Cody. At least now I could commiserate and have some laughs as well.

"HEY, SO WHERE do you think you want to go next?" Mila chugged down the last drops of her drink quickly and gave me a quick glance.

"Home," I said quickly. Even though I was enjoying our time out together, I still wanted to be that miserable person in bed, watching sad romantic movies and feeling sorry for myself as I gained ten pounds stuffing my face with candy and ice cream.

"You can't go home." Mila glared at me. "We're already out."

"Yeah, we're out, but I don't want to be out anymore."

"Sally," she whined.

"Mila, Mila, Mila, Mila." I said her name over and over again and she glared at me.

"You can be so annoying."

"Not as annoying as you can be."

"You need another drink."

"Like I need a lobotomy?" I asked with a small smile. "No thanks."

"Sally."

"Just stop. I don't want another drink and I don't want to go to another crappy bar," I whined, getting into my baby-girl act. "I just wanna go home."

"I promise the next bar will be a lot better."

"What's a lot better?" I cocked my head to one side and raised an eyebrow at her.

"Come and you will see."

"Why are you doing this to me? I just want to go home and sleep and drown my sorrows."

"You can drown your sorrows here with me."

"Wouldn't you rather be home with TJ, letting him tell you sweet nothings and kissing your neck?" I made a face.

"TJ doesn't whisper sweet nothings, so no. And I promised this night to you, so really you should be happy."

"Yay, you promised pitiful me a night out."

"You're not pitiful."

"Uh huh. I totally am pitiful." I made a face at her. "I'm going to start dating. I've decided."

"What do you mean?" Mila gave me a look.

"I'm going to join an online dating service, or two or three." I shrugged. "I just need to get out there and meet someone new. Or someone who is interested in doing me."

"Sally!" Mila made a face at me. "Come on now."

"What?" I looked at her and made a face back at her. "I don't want to be a single loser forever."

"You're not a single loser."

"I am. I'm a loser. I can't believe I've been trying to get Cody for this long. What have I been thinking? It's never going to happen. He's just not interested in me in that way."

"Cody is an idiot. We both know that. He doesn't know what he wants."

"I'm not waiting around for him anymore." I shook my head. "I'm done being the girl that every other girl calls a fool."

"No one is calling you a fool."

"Not anymore, because I'm moving on."

"Sally, you're being emotional."

"Well, duh. I mean, who wouldn't be in this situation?"

"I know." She nodded. "And I support you. Just don't write Cody off yet."

"He's already written me off." I rolled my eyes.

"We don't know that. Just give him a chance. No matter how many awesome guys you meet who want to sweep you off of your feet. There could be many other reasons why Cody went funny the other night. You know guys are weird, and my brother is the weirdest of them all. He probably doesn't even know what he wants. Maybe he's just trying to figure out what he's doing and what he wants."

"Mila, let's just go." I groaned. "This is making me more depressed. I don't even want to think about it anymore. I just want to forget him."

"Fine, but to another bar, okay? Let's just try one more."

"Fine." I sighed loudly and looked around me. "I doubt it could be worse than this." We stood up and I did a little shimmy as we walked out. As we reached the door, I turned back around and saw the bartender and the two older guys staring at me. I did a pirouette and then raised my hands in the air. "Peace out, y'all," I shouted into the bar and then exited, Mila following behind me and shaking her head as she laughed.

CHAPTER ELEVEN

Cody

"SO THEN THEY asked me if I wanted to be lead and of course I said yes." Louisa batted her long fake eyelashes at me and I smiled and nodded as she continued to talk about her dance roles.

"Interesting," I said as I sipped my beer, my mind wandering to Sally. I looked down at my watch. It was 8pm and I'd only been on this date for thirty minutes, but I was already bored out of my mind and wondering what Sally was up to. I hadn't been able to stop thinking about her since the other night. The taste of her skin against my lips had been sweet, mesmerizing and intoxicating. I could still remember the way her back had arched as I'd teased and tantalized her breasts. My entire body had felt like it was on fire as we'd kissed and touched each other. It had been an amazing moment and I'd ruined it. Not because I hadn't wanted to take her. Every inch of me had wanted to be inside her. Every inch of me had wanted to please her, to take her to heights that would have her screaming out my name. I'd wanted to feel her nails digging into my back until they punctured the skin, to feel her whipping her hair across my skin and face as she gyrated on top of me. I'd wanted to consume her so that her whole body would never want another man—which had scared me, and that was when I'd stopped. Drunken hookups were fine.

I had no problem with casual sex, but something about my thoughts when I was playing with Sally had made me hesitant.

"I'm also very flexible." Louisa's voice interrupted my thoughts and I looked up at her as she smiled at me in a sexy way with her bright red, vixen lips.

"Oh, really?" I nodded at her and tried to show enthusiasm at her obvious flirting. Louisa was beautiful and fit, probably better-looking than her online photos, but I just couldn't seem to drum up excitement about our date.

"Flexible is good," I said eventually. "I'm not so flexible."

"Only one of us needs to be." She giggled. "I'm flexible enough for both of us."

"Good to know." I smiled at her and watched as her bright red fingernails tapped across the table top. "Would you like to get another glass of wine?" I asked her, though I really didn't care if she said yes or no. I wanted to text Sally and see if she wanted to watch a movie or something, but I knew that would be a mistake. I didn't want to lead her on or take advantage of her. And it irritated me that I was thinking of her while on this date with Louisa.

"Sure," she said and leaned toward me. "We can have another glass here and then maybe head back to my place."

"Sure," I said with a grin. I still had it! "Waiter," I said, calling him over. "A glass of Zinfandel and a Blue Moon, please."

"Yes, sir." He nodded and walked away.

"So tell me more about you, Louisa. Any surprising stories?"

"Hmm, naughty or nice?" she said with a wink and I knew in that instant that she was mine for the taking if I wanted her. Which I wasn't quite sure I did. And frankly this annoyed me. She was a beautiful girl and I never said no to a beautiful woman. I felt my phone vibrating in my pocket and immediately my mind went to Sally. Was she texting me? I looked up and saw that Louisa was still talking to me, but all I could think about was the text. I knew that the probability of the text being from Sally was slim, but I wondered if she was thinking of me at the same time that I was thinking of her.

"Excuse me a second," I apologized to Louisa and I grabbed my phone out of my pocket. "I'm expecting an important message and I just need to check my phone. I hope you don't think I'm being horribly rude."

"Go ahead." Louisa nodded and batted her eyelashes again.

"Thanks." I grabbed my phone quickly from my pocket and checked the screen. I felt disappointed when I saw that the text was from my friend John. I didn't even bother opening the full message before turning my phone off and putting it back in my pocket. "Sorry about that."

"Was it the message you were waiting on?" Louisa asked me curiously, and I shook my head.

"It can wait," I said and leaned forward. "I don't want to be rude." I grabbed her hand and smiled at her, giving her my lopsided grin that seemed to make women swoon.

"Oh, no worries." She shrugged. "At least neither one of us had to pull the 'my friend just had a heart attack and I have to leave' stunt."

"What stunt is that?" I asked her, not sure what she was talking about.

"How many people have you met online?" she asked with a laugh. "So many guys and girls have fake or old photos or completely lie about themselves. I've had so many deaths and heart attacks occur on dates that I'm scared someone I know really will die."

"So a lot of bad dates, then?"

"You're the best one yet," she said, and her fingers squeezed mine. "When I saw you walk in, I thought I'd won the lottery."

"Oh?"

"Yeah, you're the hottest guy I've ever met online." She laughed. "Though I don't know that I should be telling you that."

"Aww, you can tell me anything you want," I said with a smile, though I was already regretting having held her hand. Her fingers felt clammy against mine and I couldn't stop myself from thinking about Sally and how soft and warm and silky her hands had felt against mine. I was driving myself crazy, or at least I had been since that night. Everything felt awkward since that night. I'd woken up the next morning and Sally had been gone. I'd felt empty inside when I realized she'd just left without saying goodbye, but I had thought everything would still be okay. But then she hadn't called or texted. At all. And that wasn't like Sally. She usually texted me several times a day with random questions and comments. It wasn't even something I'd paid attention to, until the texts had stopped. And now...well, now I wanted to know why she'd stopped. And I knew I hadn't made it better when I'd called her for advice for my date. I'd heard the shock in her voice when she'd responded to my question, the pause when she said, "You're going on a date and you want my help?" I knew it had been a dumb move, but I'd just wanted to talk to her and show her that everything was still cool. We were still friends. I still valued her opinion. Just because we'd almost had sex didn't mean anything had to change. I didn't want anything to change, but I felt like it already had.

"I'm not the sort of girl who has one-night stands," Louisa said, and her words broke me out of my reverie. I looked up at her and saw the shy, demure look on her face, and part of me wondered if this was an act.

"Good for you. I can't say the same." I laughed casually, my words being an understatement. I'd had far too many one-night stands, but really what guy hadn't? I enjoyed sex and, to me, that enjoyment was enough. It didn't mean anything to me and I was pretty sure most women understood that. Though once again that made me think of Sally. Why hadn't I just slept with her? Any other woman and I wouldn't have even have thought about stopping. But then, I'd never looked at another woman and felt the same depth of feelings as I had for Sally that night. Though, I suppose that was because she'd been in my life so long and was now one of my closest friends. I didn't want to overstep that line, that boundary that might somehow cheapen our friendship.

"I guess a guy as good-looking as you can have his pick of women," Louisa said, continuing to butter me up, and I wondered why she was laying it on so strong. She was a beautiful woman, so she certainly didn't need to be going after me this much.

"Well, I can't complain." I shrugged.

"So what are you looking for?" she continued and her eyes searched mine desperately. I was starting to feel like perhaps the reason why she was on the dating sites was more due to her intensity than anything else.

"Not really sure. More something casual," I said slowly. "I'm not really sure what I'm looking for right now."

"Hmm, I see." Louisa pulled her hand back from me and frowned. "I'm looking for a husband."

"Okay, then." I nodded at her and I could feel my stomach churning. This was so not a match. "I can honestly say I'm not ready for marriage yet." I gave her an apologetic smile.

"But maybe in the future?" she asked hopefully.

"I guess?" I shrugged, starting to feel like the conversation had taken a dangerous turn. Especially for a first date. Didn't she know these weren't the conversations to be having with men? I almost felt like laughing. Sally would think it was hilarious when

I told her what had gone down on this date, I thought to myself, and then I paused. I couldn't really call Sally and tell her anything. I wasn't sure she'd appreciate me calling to tell her about my bad date, though I knew she'd get a kick out of it.

"Look, I'm going to be honest," Louisa continued. "I'm looking for a husband. I'm not getting any younger, and I want kids, but I think you're hot. And it's been a while, so I'm willing."

"Uh, willing for what?" I asked her curiously.

"Willing to see where this goes."

"Where what goes?" I asked dumbly. Was she serious?

"I'm willing to go home with you tonight," she purred. "I've got an itch I think you can scratch."

"Oooh," I said with a grin. "I see."

"And I'm sure you have one I can scratch as well." I felt her hand under the table, rubbing my thigh and running its way up towards my crotch. I felt nothing at her touch and for a few brief seconds I felt sad. I wished I weren't even here. I wasn't having fun. I didn't want to be with her. I wanted to be hanging out with Sally. And I'd love for *her* to be rubbing me right now. I sighed as she crossed my mind again. This was getting totally ridiculous. I didn't know why I couldn't stop thinking about her, and then I bet it was because I hadn't fucked her. I thought that if I'd only slept with her, she'd be gone from my mind. I wanted to slap myself.

"I'm okay," I said and jumped up. "Hey, I have to go to the restroom. I'll be right back." I walked away from the table quickly, my head feeling heavy and confused as I went to pee. I didn't know what was wrong with me, but I knew I had to fix it fast. Maybe sleeping with Louisa was what I needed to help me stop thinking about Sally. I knew it would be a risk, since Louisa seemed all sorts of psycho and was likely to go all stalker on me, but I'd handled stalkers before. All you had to do was ignore them. They went even crazier at first, but then they finally got the hint. Especially if you told them you'd get a restraining order or something.

Though I wondered if it was worth the hassle. I didn't want to sleep with Louisa. No part of my body was interested in her. I'd probably have to think of Sally to even get off. I could feel myself growing angry at that thought. Sally was nothing but a friend to me and as soon as my big and little head realized that, I'd be okay. I exited the bathroom with one thought in my mind. I'd take Louisa to a bar and see what happened after we both had a bit more to drink. I knew it wasn't my best idea, but I knew I had to stop thinking about Sally before she drove me crazy.

"ANOTHER SHOT?" I asked Louisa as we stood by the bar, both of us already quite drunk, but not ready to leave.

"Sure, why not?" She giggled as she placed her hand on my arm. "Trying to get me intoxicated?"

"I'm not sure if I need to try," I said and she giggled some more and pressed herself against my chest.

"I'm ready to leave whenever you are," she said and then licked her lips slowly. "I'm ready to be a bad, bad girl."

"Oh?" I asked her, staring as she sucked on her pinky finger.

"A bad, bad girl," she said again, this time with more inflections.

"I see." I grinned down at her, faking an enthusiasm I didn't really feel.

"You do?" she said and I felt her hand sliding down the front of my jeans. "I can't feel it," she said with a pout as she moved her hand away. Normally a comment like that would make me feel like I had to man-up, but for some reason her overt sexual talk was doing nothing for me.

"I've never had any complaints," I said finally with a wink.

"I'm sure I wouldn't be complaining," she said and I felt her tongue in my ear.

It was then that the hairs on the back of my neck stood up and I felt a sudden chill. I wasn't sure how I knew, but I just did. I moved my head to the side and all of a sudden I saw Mila and Sally standing there, staring at me and Louisa. Sally's eyes were wide and as they met mine, I felt a flicker of worry as something akin to disappointment flashed through her eyes. I immediately stepped away from Louisa and raised my hand and waved my sister and Sally over to join us. My stomach flipped as I watched them give each other a small look and then walk over to me. I could see Sally muttering something to Mila and I would have given anything to know what she was saying.

"Fancy seeing you guys here," I said brightly and gave them both a hug.

"Hey, bro," Mila said, her eyes flashing at me.

"Hi, Cody," Sally said and looked away.

"Who's this, then?" Louisa asked me forcefully. I gave her a small smile and then turned back to the girls.

"This is Mila, my sister, and this is Sally," I said, willing Sally to look at me. "She's Mila's childhood best friend," I said and then paused. I didn't know what else to say. She's my friend? She's one of my closest friends? She's my almost lover? She's someone I have feelings for that I don't quite understand? I frowned and then looked at Louisa. "And this is Louisa."

"I'm his date," she said as she offered her hand. "Cody, I didn't expect to be meeting your family on the first date." She giggled as she looked up at me. "What's on the second date? Dinner with your parents?"

"Ha-ha," I said, not laughing, feeling annoyed with myself for having brought Louisa to this bar. "So what have you two been up to, then?" I asked both Mila and Sally the question, but my eyes were on Sally, drinking in her face.

"Drinking. Hanging out," Mila spoke, and Sally nodded.

"You guys want a drink?" I asked, offering to buy them a drink even though I knew date protocol should really have me dedicating my time to Louisa.

"Uhm, are you sure?" Mila looked at me and then at Louisa and made a face. "We don't want to interrupt your date."

"You won't be," I said with a smile, feeling annoyed at Mila. Why was she making this more difficult?

"Well, you might be ruining our style," Mila continued. "We're looking for a nice guy."

"You have TJ." I narrowed my eyes at her. "Aren't you in love with him or something?"

"I said we're looking." Mila rolled her eyes. "The guy isn't for me, obviously. He's for Sally."

"I see." I felt my stomach twisting and I looked at Sally. "You didn't tell me you were looking."

"You never really asked." She shrugged nonchalantly and looked up at me with a faint smile. Her eyes gazed into mine with an innocent look and she reminded me of a doe, all wide-eyed and nervous. What was she thinking? Was she thinking about that night? Was she mad at me? Did she hate me?

I wanted to tell her I was sorry for taking her back to my place. That I was sorry for kissing her and touching her. I wanted to tell her I hoped she didn't think I'd taken advantage of her, but more than that I wanted to tell her I'd spent the last few nights restlessly thinking of her and reliving those moments, wishing things had gone differently. I wanted to tell her I could still taste her on my lips and feel her nails on my back. I could still feel her silky strands of hair on my chest, teasing my nipples. And I could still feel her quivering body underneath mine. My mind was constantly on her, wishing I could hear her screaming out my name as I took her to heights she'd never known before. I'd thought that maybe, just maybe, she'd be thinking the same.

But no. Here she was out looking for a guy, just days after our night. That made me mad and I didn't even stop to think about what a hypocrite I was being. Here I was, also out, but actually on a date.

"So are you looking to hook up, or for more?" I asked, trying to sound casual. "Or just whatever you can get?"

"I'm just looking for a nice guy, like every other girl," Sally said softly.

"She wants a guy who can commit and show her that she's special and treat her like a Queen," Mila said sharply. "She wants a guy who will be there for her and love her and dedicate his life to her."

"And you guys came here?" I asked questioningly. "Really?"

"Are you saying only the shady guys come here?" Mila gave me a pointed look and I glared at her. Why was she trying to force Sally into something?

"That's not what I'm saying." I shook my head. "I just think Sally can meet a higher quality guy than the guys who are here tonight."

"You guys don't have to talk about me like I'm not here," Sally broke in and put her hands up. "I'm here and just looking to have fun."

"Same here." Louisa pouted and grabbed my arm. "I thought we were going to go back to your place and have some real fun, big boy?" Everyone went quiet at her words and I looked over at Sally to see how she'd react. Her face was downcast and she wouldn't make eye contact with me. I tried not to sigh. This was a mess, and I didn't know how to fix it.

"We'll let you guys be, then," Mila said, giving me a disappointed look. "Sally and I can take care of ourselves and our drinks for the night."

"Mila," I said, annoyed. "I want to buy you guys your first drinks."

"We don't want to interrupt you on your big night, Cody," Sally spoke up and looked at me coldly. "Louisa doesn't want her first date with you to also include her sister and her friend."

"You're my friend as well," I said softly, gazing into her eyes, wanting to pull her into me and kiss her.

"Yeah, yeah," she said and pursed her lips.

"What does that mean?" My voice grew louder and I stepped toward her. "We're friends, right?"

"Yeah, of course." She gave me a big smile that didn't reach her eyes. "We're great friends."

"Why does that sound insincere?"

"Cody, let her be." Mila sounded annoyed. "We're here to have fun. Sally needs to get laid."

"WHAT?" I practically shouted and I felt like fire was shooting from my eyes.

"I'm joking." Mila gave me a weird look. "Calm down."

"I'm calm," I said and then looked at Sally. "So maybe we can go to lunch tomorrow?"

"I'm busy." She shook her head. "Sorry."

"I see." I frowned. 'Busy doing *what?* I wanted to ask her, but I didn't.

"Cody, are you nearly done?" Louisa tapped me on the shoulder impatiently. "I want to get out of here."

"Yeah, just a second." I sighed and tried not to roll my eyes. "What about this weekend?"

"Sally's coming over for lunch," Mila said. "You should

come too. We'll make it a nice family affair."

"Fine," I said with a small frown. I didn't want to do lunch with TJ and Mila. I wanted to talk to Sally alone. I wanted to make sure everything between us was okay and I wanted to find out what the hell she was doing going to bars looking for other guys. "I'll be there."

"Whoop dee doo." Mila grabbed Sally's arm and then looked at me. "Have a good night, Cody. We'll see you later."

"Night," I said reluctantly and watched as she dragged Sally across the bar and stood next to two athletic-looking guys who immediately started looking at them. I could feel my body growing hot as I watched them standing there studying Sally. I wondered if she was into them. I wondered if she would be dumb enough to fall for their lines. I wondered if she would go home with one of them. My heart stopped at the thought and I looked away quickly.

"I'm ready to leave now," Louisa said, staring at me, and I looked down at her in surprise, already having forgotten she was there.

"I'll give you money for a cab," I said quickly as I pulled out my wallet. "I forgot that I have things to do tonight."

"Oh?" She looked put out and pissed off, but I didn't care.

"This should cover it." I handed her a couple of twenties. "I'll walk with you to get a cab if you want."

"Don't put yourself out," she said, but I was barely listening to her. My eyes were on Sally and the jock who had just started talking to her. I felt my skin growing cold as she threw her head back and laughed at something he'd said. What the hell was so funny?

"What is your problem, dude?" Louisa pushed past me and I realized she was leaving. I stared over at Sally flirting with the random guy and then at Louisa as she walked away. I didn't want to leave the bar, but I knew I wouldn't be a gentleman if I let Louisa leave without making sure she'd gotten into a taxi safely, so I quickly followed behind her. I'd have to be quick though, because I was definitely going to come back to the bar, just to make sure Mila and Sally were safe and not taken advantage of by the two guys they were talking to, who were looking shadier and shadier by the minute.

CHAPTER TWELVE

Sally

"SO WHAT YOU up to tonight?" Cody asked me nonchalantly as we waited on Mila and TJ to bring out the lunch. His eyes bore into mine with an intense expression and I wondered what he was thinking. Everything was even more awkward between us since that night we'd nearly made love and the night we'd met up when he'd been on his date. We hadn't spoken since that night, and I wasn't really sure exactly what he was thinking. All I knew was I had to move on. Seeing him on that date with Louisa had been the nail in the coffin for me. It was then that I'd realized I had to move on. Like, really move on. Cody felt nothing for me, and if he did, he was just playing games. It didn't—I didn't—mean anything to him. Not like he meant to me. I needed to just forget about all of my daydreams and hopes. I couldn't afford to live the rest of my life pining away for him.

"Not really sure," I lied, not wanting to tell Cody I had a date. I was already a nervous wreck and part of me felt like telling Cody about the date would be like slamming the door on our non-existent relationship. And that would mean I would be giving up all hope. And while I knew I was a fool for having hope in the first place, it was a hard thing to give up. I just really wanted to believe that maybe someday it could happen. Even though I knew I was moving on from him, it was still hard to shut the door completely. I wanted to cry as I sat there, hating myself for being so flimsy and weak. I'd just told myself I was going to move on from him, yet I still wasn't able to completely make the change.

"I'm going to go check out a band in the fashion district if you want to come," he said casually as he sipped some water.

"Oh? Who?" My heart thudded excitedly. Was he asking me out? I felt myself about to say yes when I realized that in order to accept his very casual invitation, I'd have to ditch my date with Luke. And while I didn't have the same feeling for Luke, he seemed like a really genuine guy who could really like and be into me. And, well, that meant a whole lot more than what Cody was offering. He barely knew what I did for a living. And he never really showed any huge interest in me aside from casual hanging out.

"I can't remember the name." He shrugged. "But it's free and I think it's sponsored by some brewery, so lots of cheap and free beer."

"Oh, I see. Who else is going?"

"I'm not sure. Some of my buddies and then some girls we met at the bar last week."

"Oh?" My stomach dropped and I was glad I hadn't dropped my plans and said I was going to go. I didn't want to be around him and more girls that were all over him talking about their plans for the night.

"So, yeah, feel free to come." He shrugged and then stretched his arms. "Mila, where is this food?" he shouted aloud. "Are you trying to make me starve tonight?"

"Cody, shut-it," she shouted back at him, and I laughed. "It'll be ready soon."

"So, I don't think I can make it tonight," I said softly and gazed at him, everything in me wanting him to look sad and beg me to come. Even though I knew he wouldn't.

"Okay." He nodded and gave me a smile, no sadness in his eyes or face. As if it meant nothing to him. Which it likely didn't. Because I meant nothing to him.

"I have a date," I said, hoping that maybe that would strike something in him, maybe some sort of jealousy. I knew it was a long shot. I knew I was playing with fire, but I wanted to affect him. I wanted to hurt him. I wanted him to feel one iota of the jealousy and confusion that I was feeling. How could he not feel it?

"Cool, good for you. Anyone I know?" He tilted his head, his eyes narrowing slightly, the smile still on his face.

"You don't know him. His name is Luke," I continued, my heart feeling like it was breaking. How could I be so upset about going on a date with someone? I knew I wasn't upset about the date, but more so that Cody wasn't reacting in the way I wanted him to. Why was he smiling like it was a good thing? Why didn't he look pissed or upset? Didn't he care at all?

"Luke Skywalker?" he said with a laugh, and I shook my head.

"No. Not Luke Skywalker."

"So, how did you guys meet?" he asked me again. This time his voice was tight and his eyes were a little colder. I gazed back at him and for a second part of me wanted to ask him if he really cared or if he was just asking to ask.

"I actually met him through a girl at work." I smiled, not knowing why I was lying. Maybe I felt like I was a loser admitting I'd met him online. "He came to a happy hour with her boyfriend and we kinda hit it off."

"Wow, look at you. Just reeling them in."

"Oh, yeah, that's me. I get all the guys—hook, line and

sinker."

"Well, that's why you pretty girls always have it easier than us men."

"Ha, yeah, okay." I laughed, though I was on cloud nine that he'd called me pretty. Why was I so pitiful?

"So what does he do?"

"I can't really remember. I guess I'll find out tonight." I laughed. "I was a little tipsy when we met, but he seems like a really nice guy. Really friendly, really funny, really sweet." I knew I was laying it on thick, but I wasn't sure what else to say.

"Friendly, funny and sweet?" Cody's facial expression was almost stoic now. "Is that all you girls look for now?"

"Well, you know." I laughed, feeling suddenly better that he wasn't looking so happy. "He's super-hot as well."

"Because super-hot means a lot, right?" he said with a sneer.

"Oh, yeah, it means everything to me." I rolled my eyes. "All my boyfriends need to be super-hot."

"So he's your boyfriend now?"

"I hardly think so." I rolled my eyes at him. "This is technically our first date. We've only met once before this."

"So maybe after tonight he'll be your boyfriend? Or do you need multiple dates for that to happen?"

"For what to happen? What are you going on about, Cody?" I asked him in confusion. "You're not really making much sense."

"I'm just helping you think about what you want. The important questions," he said with a frown. "How long will it take for you guys to be an official couple?"

"I have no idea. I don't even know if he's interested."

"I guess ask him tonight."

"I'm not going to ask him that. That's ridiculous. I would look crazy. Who asks someone if they want to be boyfriend/girlfriend after one date?"

"You're not asking him that specific question, you're asking him how many dates it will take for him to consider that relationship with you."

"I'm not asking him either of those questions."

"Why not?"

"Why are you being so ridiculous, Cody?" I frowned. "I barely know this guy. I'm not going to ask him anything about relationships. I'm not desperate."

"Okay, sure. If you say so."

"Yeah, I say so." I was annoyed.

"I mean, I know you really want to meet someone."

"What's that supposed to mean?" I sat up straight and my tone changed.

"I mean, now that Mila is getting married, I suppose your biological clock is ticking."

"You're an asshole."

"I'm just telling the truth as I see it."

"You see me as some desperado who is dying to get married? Is that what you're saying?"

"Would I say that?" He gave me a huge grin. "I mean, would I call you a desperado?"

"Yeah, I think you would." I didn't grin back, my feelings super hurt.

"I'm just joking, Sally. I hope your date with Luke goes well and if you guys want to come join us at the concert later, just let me know."

"Yeah, I'll see."

"What are you guys doing, anyway?"

"I think dinner and a movie?"

"Movie?" He made a face. "That's not a good first date option. What talking can you do there?"

"It's an art-house movie. I think he said he wanted to grab a coffee afterwards and discuss."

"Boring."

"Cody!" I admonished him, but laughed slightly as I did think the date sounded a bit lame. I mean, I liked movies, but what exactly was an art-house movie and what were we going to be discussing afterwards? I wasn't sure I even knew what to look for in the movie and I was hoping I didn't fall asleep.

"I just hope you don't fall asleep on the guy," he said and our eyes met for a few seconds. I wondered if he could read my mind. Wondered if he knew that all he needed to say was he didn't want me to go—and the date would be done. Wondered if he knew he was the only guy I wanted to fall asleep on, in more ways than one.

"Yeah, I don't anticipate that happening," I said and waited for him to say something, anything that would be a real indication that I shouldn't be attempting to move on.

"Good, you want to make a good impression." He grinned at me then and rubbed his stomach. "Man, I'm so hungry."

"Yeah, me too." I nodded at him, realizing that the conversation about my date was over. And I felt like I was the only one who was feeling bad about everything. He didn't seem hurt or jealous, and that was actually making me feel worse inside. Why couldn't he just feel the same way I did? Why couldn't he love me? Why couldn't he just, for one second, react in the way I wanted him to? I just didn't know how to get rid of these feelings. I didn't know how to stop loving him. I just wanted to cry. I just wanted to go home and lie in my bed and feel sorry for myself. I didn't even want to go on the date with Luke anymore. Yes, I was attracted to his photos, but not in the same way I was to Cody in real life. Just seeing Cody made my heart skip a beat. I wasn't sure if it was healthy—well, I knew it wasn't healthy. I

knew I was obsessed. I knew I was driving myself crazy. That I
was making myself sick and depressed. I knew I was in the worst
possible position that I could be in, in this situation. I knew, at
the bottom of my heart, that I needed to let go of Cody. I
couldn't keep going through this. I needed to stop feeling this
way. It was just breaking my heart. Every time I saw him, I
wanted to cry. Well, not when I saw him. It was always after I
saw him. Always when the emptiness hit me. That was when I
wanted to cry and curl up inside of myself. I just couldn't take it
anymore. I didn't want to feel this way anymore. I didn't want
to be so depressed that I couldn't sleep. I didn't want my dreams
to be filled with him. I didn't want my every waking moment to
be filled with wishing I could be with him.

Sometimes I felt like I was wishing upon a star—a sad, lone-
ly, low-hanging star. A star that shone so brightly, had so much
hope, seemed so close, but when I reached up, it was always just
out of my grasp. Always just a little too far away. I wanted to
believe that one day I'd get there, that I'd be able to hold it in
my hands, but it was elusive, ever elusive, and I didn't know if I
had the time or energy for *one day* anymore. I just didn't know
what the point was. One day a million things could happen. One
day I could be dead. One day, one day, one day nothing could
happen. One day, I could wake up and realize I'd wasted my
whole life reaching for something that was always just out of
reach. I knew that today was the day I had to change. I needed to
be done with the games. I needed to be done with the dreams
and the hopes. I needed to just be done. I needed to take care of
the heart that was breaking inside of me. I needed to heal. If I
didn't, I wasn't sure I wouldn't sink into an even deeper hole. A
hole that I'd never get out of. And that scared me more than a
life without Cody. I couldn't keep living like this. I had finally
come to the realization that I had to give up. I just didn't know

how.

"By the way," I said, needing to come clean, "I lied. I met him online. We've exchanged a few emails, but this will be the first time we're meeting." I gave Cody a crooked smile. "But you're right, Mila getting engaged to TJ has made me realize I want a serious boyfriend. I want someone to love me who I can love back. I don't think that's too much to ask."

"It's not," he said slowly, his eyes never leaving mine as he gave me a small, weak smile. "I think you deserve the best, Sally. You really do."

"Thank you," I said, my heart breaking.

"I hope he's a great guy," he continued. "I hope you fall in love and he can be the man you need and want. I hope you find everything you're looking for. You're a great girl and you deserve the best."

"Thanks," I said, my heart being torn out of my body at his words. All hope had left the building. It had hit me once again. Cody didn't love me. He never would. He didn't care. At all. He never would. My heart sank with a thousand ships and my spirit left me. It was all I could do to keep a smile on my face as we sat there, both of us looking away and fiddling with our cutlery as we waited for Mila and TJ to bring out our lunch.

CHAPTER THIRTEEN

Cody

I WANTED TO punch someone or break something. All through lunch all I could think about was Sally going on her date with Luke. What sort of name was *Luke*? I could already tell by his name that he was a loser. Sally could do way better than him. And dinner and a movie? And discussing the movie at a coffee shop afterwards? What was that, some sort of new code for getting her to his place so he could try and sleep with her? I hoped Sally was smarter than that. This guy was trying to Netflix and chill her by using some sort of high-class tactic. At least girls I slept with knew the deal. I wasn't trying to pretend I was going to make them my wife. They knew that a hookup was a hookup. And nine out of ten times it was at their place, so I didn't have to worry about them becoming a stage-five clinger and hanging out at my place the next day. There was nothing worse than a hookup trying to stay the night and then waking up to them cooking me breakfast the next day. That was always awkward for me. Sometimes I couldn't even remember their names. I knew it was bad, but it wasn't like I lied to them. They knew the deal. Sex was sex. What guy turned down sex? Well, me—once. But that had been different. That had been with Sally. And, well, I couldn't just do casual sex with her.

"Lunch was delicious. Thank you, Mila." Sally beamed at my

sister after finishing her cheesecake and I watched as she folded her napkin and placed it next to her plate on the table. She gazed at me for a second, gave me a quick smile and then looked away. "I think I should get going soon. I've a lot to do today."

"Oh?" I said, feeling annoyed for some reason. "Need to get ready for your date?"

"Yeah, kinda." She nodded, looking slightly embarrassed.

"Let me give you some advice. Guys prefer a more natural look, so maybe stay away from too much makeup, and no slutty clothes."

"Cody." Mila's voice was sharp. "What the hell?"

"I'm just giving Sally some pointers."

"Are you saying I normally wear too much makeup and slutty clothes?" Sally's voice was unsure.

"No, I mean, I'm sure every woman has at some point. I'm just saying don't wear them tonight. And don't be a fool and go back to his place to listen to music or whatever. Because he doesn't want you to listen to music, he wants to get you in bed. And that means one thing."

"Okay," Sally said simply. I could feel TJ and Mila staring at me, but I couldn't stop talking.

"And I know you want a relationship, so honestly, having sex on the first through fifth date is not a good idea. The guy just won't look at you the same way."

"So that's something you live by, then, Cody?" Mila asked me sarcastically. "That's your dating philosophy as well?"

"I'm not looking to get married or have kids." I shrugged. "At least not anytime soon. So if I'm hooking up, that's all I care about."

"Good to know," Mila said and stood up abruptly. "Anyone want any cheese and crackers?" she said as she glared at me.

"Sure," TJ said with a nod.

"I'll help you," Sally said and stood up quickly as well and they both left the room hastily. I looked over at TJ, who was grinning widely at me, and I frowned.

"What?" I asked him, wondering what he found so amusing.

"Dude, *what* are you doing?" He leaned forward and spoke softly.

"What do you mean what am I doing?"

"What's with the rude advice to Sally?" He shook his head. "'Don't wear too much makeup'?"

"I was just telling her how it is from our side. You know, I'm looking out for her."

"Are you falling for her?" His eyes narrowed as he gazed at me.

"What?" I looked at him like he was crazy. "Of course not."

"Uh huh."

"Dude, we almost had sex last week and I stopped it, okay?" I lowered my voice as I spoke. "If I wanted her, I could have hit it and quit it and moved on already."

"No, you couldn't have, and maybe the reason you didn't is because you like her." TJ's blue eyes looked into mine intensely.

"I'm telling you that I like her as a friend. She's Mila's best friend and, well, we've become a lot closer recently as well. I consider her a good friend."

"Really, dude?"

"Really." I nodded. "That's it. I mean, yeah, she's pretty and she's pretty awesome, but you know me, I don't do relation-ships."

"I know you don't." He shook his head. "But I'm telling you this as a friend—if you have feelings for Sally, you'd better act on them soon. And if you don't, don't play around with her anymore."

"I'm not playing around with her." I glared at him. "What

sort of man do you think I am?"

"I know how it can be, Cody." TJ made a face at me. "When I started falling for Mila, it was really hard for me to accept. I never saw myself as this guy who could fall in love and want to be with one woman forever, but I learned to accept that I was."

"Dude, we're not the same. Also, you were sleeping with my sister." I glared at him. "You were already taking advantage of her, so I'm glad you manned-up, because you know I would have had to kill you if you hadn't."

"Look, I'm just saying that I think we've all noticed your hostility when it comes to Sally and other guys and, well personally, I think there's only one reason for that."

"I'm not in love with Sally." I shook my head vehemently. "I'm trying to be a good friend to her. I want her to meet a good guy," I said, though inside I wasn't sure I was ready for her to actually start dating someone seriously. I didn't know what that said about me and how I felt, though I knew I didn't love her or anything.

"You can tell yourself what you want, Cody, but I'm just letting you know what it looks like from this side. Just don't ignore your feelings until it's too late." TJ shrugged. "I know you see yourself as the ultimate playboy, but sometimes you need to dig a little deeper."

"Dig a little deeper?" I laughed. "What is this, a sermon from the Oprah Winfrey show?"

"You're an idiot." TJ shook his head at me and laughed. "I'm just telling you man-to-man, I don't know that Sally's going to be single forever and I don't want you to wake up one day and think to yourself that she's the one who got away."

"Trust me, bro, it's not like that," I said, starting to feel annoyed. It was at that moment that Mila and Sally walked back in the room with the cheese and crackers. I looked up into Sally's laughing face and studied her long black hair and big brown eyes, her lips wide as she laughed, and for a few seconds her smile was turned toward me, her eyes gazing deeply into mine with a happy expression, and I felt my mood lifting. She was so beautiful. It was a pity we wanted different things. I knew in that instant I didn't want her going on a first date with Luke. I didn't want her sleeping with him, but I knew that was selfish of me. I wasn't looking for anything more than casual.

Sally and Mila sat down then, and I found myself leaning forward and resting my hand on Sally's leg under the table. I wasn't sure why I felt the need to touch her, but I did.

"Cody?" she said and looked at me with a hesitant smile as my hand moved up her leg slowly.

"Yes?" I said with a smile, teasing her.

"Cheese?" she said, her eyes asking me a question she didn't dare ask out loud as my hand slid up under her skirt.

"Sure." I nodded, my fingers finding their way to her panties. I felt her shifting in her chair and I tried not to laugh. I rubbed gently against her bud and I could feel her panties growing wet. I felt a surge of power running through my body as my fingers increased their pace. I felt powerful and happy. *Let her remember this moment when she's on her date with Luke.*

"So, do you know what movie Luke will be taking you to tonight?" Mila asked Sally, and I could feel myself growing pissed again at the fact he was being brought up.

"No, not sure," Sally said softly. "Something he really likes, though. He said he knew one of the cinematographers or something."

"Impressive," Mila said, and Sally nodded.

"Yeah, I'm really excited." She smiled. "I think it will be fun."

"Sounds like a lot of fun," I said simply and then slipped my fingers inside the side of her panties so that I was touching her, skin to skin. She gasped and her legs tightened as I rubbed her even more intimately now, her panties pushing my fingers close against her as I continued to play with her. "I'm sure you and Luke will really hit it off," I continued as I tried to slip a finger inside of her. Unfortunately, given our position, I couldn't, but that didn't stop me from trying.

"Yeah, thanks." Sally glanced at me, a bedazzled look on her face, and I felt her hand coming down on mine and tugging gently to remove it from her panties. I rubbed her for a few seconds more until she was even wetter and then I withdrew my fingers and sat back. I stared at her face for a few seconds and smiled. She was flushed and her lower lip was quivering. I knew she must be horny as hell right now. Shit, I was horny as hell. I wanted to make sure that tonight, while she was on her date, she was thinking of me.

"Actually, come with me real quick." I jumped up, not even thinking about what I was doing.

"Huh?" she asked me with a confused expression.

"I owe you an apology for the way I was talking to you earlier." I looked at her and then at Mila and TJ. "I'd like to apologize in private, if you don't mind."

"Oh, that's okay," she said and smiled weakly. "I know you were just trying to help."

"I was, but I'd love to just say some things in private, if you don't mind. Get some stuff off of my chest."

"Oh, sure?" she said and stood up.

"Excuse us?" I looked at Mila and TJ and I could see Mila's eyes were narrowed.

"Now, Cody?" she questioned me. "You want to do this now?"

"Yes, I do." I nodded and turned away from her. "We'll go

to the spare bedroom to talk." I grabbed Sally's hand and pulled her out of the room before anyone else could say anything.

"Why are we going to the spare bedroom?" Sally asked me as I pulled her into the room and closed the door. "Why not the living room?"

"Because there's no privacy in the living room," I said as I locked the door behind me.

"Why do we need privacy?" she said, just staring at me, licking her lips nervously. "And by the way, what do you think you were doing just now? You can't just touch me like that."

"I thought you liked it?" I said and pulled her over to the bed.

"Cody, I don't understand…" Her voice trailed off and I pushed her back so that she was on the mattress. "What are you doing?"

"Shh. I told you I want to apologize," I said and I pulled her skirt up quickly.

"Cody?" She gasped as I pulled her panties down.

"Shh," I said again before burying my face between her legs and working my tongue inside of her. She was still wet and her legs were trembling as they gripped my face. I licked and sucked and I could feel her body writhing on the bed underneath me as I brought her to orgasm with my tongue. I felt her hands in my hair as I worked my magic and I knew that she wanted this just as bad as I did.

"Cody, oh my," she cried out as she came.

"Shh." I placed a finger on her lips and grinned down at her. "They'll hear you." I laughed as she gazed up at me with wide, lusty eyes. I reached down and unbuckled my belt and pulled my hardness out. Her eyes widened as she gazed at my cock and I positioned myself between her legs. "Is this okay?" I said, and she nodded. I eased myself inside of her quickly, loving how she felt around me, so warm and silky. I rested my arm on the bed next to her shoulder and kissed her as I slid in and out of her, thrusting deeper and deeper with every move. I could hear her moans of pleasure as I grunted, my body enjoying every moment of being inside of her. "Fuck, you feel good," I whispered in her ear as she squeezed her legs around my waist. "I was an idiot for not fucking you the other night," I muttered as I felt my orgasm building up. I was going to come soon and I wished I'd rubbed one out before taking her. I didn't want her to think I couldn't last long.

"Oh, my God, I think I'm going to come again." Sally moaned against my lips and so I started thrusting into her even faster.

"Are you on anything?" I groaned as I felt myself about to blow.

"No." She shook her head, her eyes wide as she stared up at me.

"Damn," I groaned, wanting to come inside of her. I thrust a few more times and then pulled out quickly and came on the side of her leg. "Sorry," I whispered down at her. "It was the quickest place."

"It's okay." She nodded and I could see from her face that she hadn't come a second time. I reached my fingers down to her wetness and immediately started rubbing her clit as I stuck two fingers inside of her. Her eyes closed and I felt her body bucking as she immediately came for me.

"Did you like that?" I said as I kissed her again, enjoying the feel of her body shaking under mine.

"I don't know what to say." She opened her eyes and looked up at me.

"You don't have to say anything," I said with a wink. "All you have to do is think of this moment when you're on your date with Luke tonight. If he asks you to come over, just say no. He won't be able to do to you the things that I do," I said as I ran my fingers over her clit one last time and then pulled her panties up and skirt down.

"What?" she said and blinked at me, looking slightly shocked at my words.

"Nothing. Sorry." I groaned as I pulled her off of the bed, my brain screaming at me. What had I just done? Had I really just fucked Sally in my sister's bedroom so that she wouldn't sleep with her date tonight? "We shouldn't have done this."

"It was your decision." She blinked at me.

"Sorry," I groaned. "I just couldn't resist you. This is my fault. I don't want to ruin anything with you and Luke."

"I don't even know what to say." Sally looked at me with a hurt expression, her eyes glistening with unshed tears.

"I'm sorry." I pulled her into my arms, my body wanting to take her again already. "I knew this would be a bad idea. I didn't mean to mess anything up."

"You didn't," she said stiffly. "It's fine."

"I know you want a relationship," I said, not able to look at her. "And it sounds like this Luke can give it to you."

"Yeah." She nodded.

"I just needed you to know what I could give you, too," I said, knowing I'd been selfish. "I needed you to know what it felt like to have me inside of you. Maybe I wanted to ensure that tonight, at least, you wouldn't be fucking anyone else."

"I'm going to go now, Cody." Sally's voice sounded distant. "You're too confusing and I can't do this anymore. I'm going to go." She pulled away from me and I watched as she walked to the bedroom door and unlocked it and walked out. I stood there, even as I heard her calling out to Mila and TJ that she was leaving. I remained standing there, even as I heard her opening the front door and exiting the apartment. I stood there until TJ came into the room and looked at me with narrowed eyes.

"What did you do?" he asked me with a frown and all I could do was shake my head. I had no idea what I'd just done, but I knew deep inside that I felt awful about it.

CHAPTER FOURTEEN

Sally

THERE'S A MOMENT when your heart stops. Sometimes it's in happiness and sometimes it's in pain. The painful moment—that's the moment I hate the most. I call this moment "the moment before living death." It's the point where you think you won't be able to go on. I've experienced that moment several times now. Every time Cody gave me a look and then turned away without really looking at me. Every time I hoped he would tell me he loved me, but he talked about another girl instead. Every time I think of him with someone else. Those moments make me want to die. The pain is so sharp, so deep, that I can feel my entire body succumbing to some unknown pain that pierces my soul. I can literally feel a piece of my soul leaving me every time he gazes away from me.

Those moments were fleeting. Up until now. Now, the moment was embedded in me. Now, the pain of near death was ingrained in my soul. I ran out of Mila's house with my entire body shaking. I was still high from Cody making love to me. I could still feel his kisses as he entered me. I could still feel the excitement and hope in my veins. The hope that had been living in me for years. The hope that he had just extinguished by telling me he still wanted me to go on the date with Luke. He hadn't slept with me because he wanted me all to himself. He hadn't slept with me because he couldn't stand me going out with Luke. He had slept with me because he didn't want sloppy seconds. He wanted to fuck me. As he'd said so crudely. And that was it. He'd taken what he'd wanted and discarded me. Told me to move on to the next guy. And yet, somewhere inside of me, there was still hope. I couldn't believe it. I couldn't believe I was such a fool. How could I be such a fool? After everything. After leaving Mila's in a panic, almost in tears, hating him with all my heart. Even when I said I was done. It was still there. I could feel it in the bottom of my soul. The hope was going to murder me in the night.

The hope is too much. It kills me—slays me in the middle of the night when I'm lying there, thinking of and rehearing our entire conversation from the day. I think about our texts, our calls, every little thing he'd said to me or hadn't said to me. Over and over again. I just don't understand how I can feel something so deep and strong. I can't fathom how my heart and soul can carry such love when there is nothing being given back to me.

I used to think it was better to have loved and lost. I used to think I was glad to be experiencing this emotion. It meant I was living and trying. Love was a good thing. Love was a beautiful thing. I used to enjoy the feeling of my heart racing every time I saw him. It used to feel like I was flying. It used to feel like I was on top of the world. I craved the feeling. At least I did when I hadn't felt the pain and the rejection. When I just lived for the moments of us being together. When a simple hello could make my week. Those were the days, the weeks, the months that made me *love* being in love. But then I got older, wiser, and sadder. Now the love is tinged in pain. Now every time we share a smile, I don't know whether I want to laugh or cry. Sometimes I feel like I can't breathe. Sometimes I feel like I can't go on. Sometimes I feel like I'm a walking corpse and that my life will never be the same again. And now that I'd slept with him, now that I'd known him in a way I'd dreamt of for years, I knew everything would only get harder.

Cody Brookstone. The man of my dreams. The man I considered my soul mate. Once upon a time I believed we were destined to be with each other. Once upon a time, I thought it was inevitable. I'd believed there could be no feeling this strong, this powerful, that wasn't real, that didn't mean we were made for each other. But now...now I'm older. Now I'm walking down the street after the best and worst moment of my life. Now, I'm sitting here on a random street bench trying not to cry my eyes out, and I'm wondering to myself what's possessed me? What's come over me? How can I be so sad, so desperate, and so crazy over someone who doesn't care?

I didn't know if he ever thought about me, if he ever cared. *Oh*, the pain at that feeling. The pain knowing he was always in my thoughts but I was nothing to him. It consumed me. Absolutely consumed me. It made me question my sanity and self-worth. It made me question everything. He meant everything to me.

I'd given myself to him willingly, lovingly. I'd been excited when he'd teased me under the table and taken me to the bedroom. I'd thought it meant something more than it had— but of course, I'd been wrong again.

I felt the warm tears running down my face and I buried my face in my hands. I let the tears pour down my face ungracefully. I let myself sob until my eyes hurt. I let my body shake. I let myself cry out in anguish. I let myself release all of the sorrow and despair that I felt. Cody had broken me. I'd let him break me. I was no longer a person I recognized. I was no longer me. And if I was honest with myself, I knew it wasn't Cody's fault. It was mine. He'd never pretended to offer me anything else. He'd never made any false promises. He'd never told me he loved me or even liked me in a way more than friends. It had all been in my head, and I had to let go. If I didn't, I was scared about how much lower I could go.

As I sat up and looked at the empty road in front of me, I realized I was already at the lowest I'd ever been and I couldn't allow myself to sink even further. It was time for me to be strong. It was time for me to let Cody go.

I HATE FIRST dates. I hate having nerves. I hate the feeling of not knowing what the guy will think of me. I hate not having confidence. I'm not really sure when or how I lost it. I think I lost it at some point around the time I realized I was in love with Cody and he didn't feel the same way about me. It took the wind out of my sails and I've never really recovered from that. I've never gotten back that hopeful innocence and self-esteem. In fact, most times now I wish I could change who I was. That's what loving Cody has done to me. It's made me wish I could change and be the woman he would fall in love with. I wish I could mold myself into the woman he wants. I'd change everything I needed to change in order for him to want me. I know that sounds pitiful. I know it's weak, but that's how much I love him. I'd change anything and everything: my looks, my personality, my likes, everything. I know that's not healthy. I know that's not love. I know I have a problem. Some deep, dark, emotional issues that I should fix. But how can I fix them? Fixing them would mean not loving Cody. It would mean acknowledging that it's never going to happen. That's hard, but I'm going to try. Mila thinks I'm going on these dates to make Cody jealous. She thinks I'm still going for his heart. But that's not completely true. While it's true that I still love him and want him with every part of me, I also want to let him go. I don't want to play these games. I don't want to be his best friend. I don't want to wake up at 3 am anymore in a dead panic. I don't want to feel like I'm not in control. It's a helpless feeling. A mind-numbing, crazy, crazy feeling. It's a feeling of emptiness that I've never experienced before. My whole life is on edge. And I hate it.

So that's why I'm really going on the date. I want to meet someone else. And that's why I'm willing to suck up my fear. Any pain or rejection I feel will be nothing compared to what I've already experienced with Cody. Rejection is a bitch. And if Luke doesn't like me, it will sting, but not as much as the pain resonating through me at what Cody has done to me. Mila thinks I'm dating as a way to win Cody, but I know that I'm dating as a way to move on. I want to find someone who can love me in the way I want to be loved. I deserve that and I know I deserve it, but I also know getting to that part is going to suck.

I checked my face in my rearview mirror one more time, reapplied some lipstick, and then jumped out, smoothing out my dress and tucking my hair back behind my ear. I took a deep breath and hurried toward the coffee shop where I was going to meet Luke. I was surprised that my eyes looked clear even after all of my earlier crying. I felt a bit weird to be going on a first date the same day I'd slept with someone else, but I was just going to pretend that Cody and I had never hooked up. I was not going to let him ruin my date with Luke.

I walked in hesitantly, surprisingly not feeling as many nerves as I thought I would. I looked around and immediately I saw him on a couch, a huge smile on his face as he jumped up.

"Hi, Sally?" he said as he walked toward me, all six feet and two inches of him looking devastatingly handsome. I looked at him in surprise. He was much better-looking than his photos, and his warm smile made me feel super happy. He made me feel like he was excited to see me. And that was something I hadn't felt from a guy in a while.

"Yes, Luke?" I smiled at him and his big brown eyes glanced into mine with such a caring look that I felt a part of me relax in a carefree way.

"That's me." He reached his hand out, then looked at me, shook his head and gave me a small smile. "Would it be awkward if I hugged you?" He made a little face, but still leaned in to hug me. I hugged him back, enjoying the warmth of his body next to mine. "Or rather, can I hug you?"

"Not awkward, and sure." I laughed as he released me and he gave me a bashful grin.

"I suppose I should have asked you and then waited for your answer first." He shook his head in a self-deprecating way and I just smiled. "Would you like a drink? Tea, coffee, hot chocolate?" He waved his arms around. "Anything you want?"

"Anything I want?" I leaned and tilted my head to the side. "What if I want a lemon drop with gold flakes?"

"Then I'm in trouble." He grinned back at me and we both laughed. I was surprised by how at ease I felt with him. "Maybe a lemonade with brown sugar that we pretend is gold?"

"That could work, I suppose." I smiled back at him.

"Thanks for meeting me here before the movie, by the way. I know I changed the plans slightly and I feel bad, but I thought that dinner might be better after the movie." He grinned bashfully. "If you still want to hang out with me by then."

"Haha, no worries. I'm flexible," I said. "I'm excited to see the movie."

"I hope you enjoy it. I realize that maybe it's not the best first date." He made a face. "Sorry. I guess I'm not a good dater."

"It's fine." I laughed. "I'm not a good dater either, so I guess we're in good company."

"I guess I got lucky, then." He gave me a lopsided smile and once again his brown eyes looked into mine warmly.

"Oh?"

"To find someone I'm so compatible with," he said and then ran his hands through his dark locks. "Now, let's get you a drink."

"Sure, thanks." I nodded and followed him to the line. I stared up at the menu and looked at my options.

"Know what you want? I recommend their vanilla lattes," he said after a minute or so.

"Sure, I'll try that." I smiled at him.

"Want to share a blueberry muffin as well?" he asked with a hopeful smile, and I just grinned as I nodded. He placed the order and we walked over to the table in the corner that he'd saved for us. "I hope this is okay," he said as he waited for me to sit. "Sorry, I don't know why I'm so nervous. Actually, I do," He grinned at me. "When I saw your profile online I was shocked to find someone as cool as you, and now meeting you in person has me wondering if I'm in a dream or something."

"Really, why?" I asked him in surprise as I sat down and sipped on my vanilla latte, which was indeed delicious.

"Because you're even prettier in person, but more than that. You have a really sweet aura about you. Does that sound weird?" He made a face. "Do I sound like some crazy hippy New-Age person?"

"No, that sounds nice. Thank you. I think you have a cool aura yourself." I grinned at him, and he laughed.

"So, Sally, tell me about you." He leaned forward.

"What do you want to know?" I smiled at him, feeling really and truly happy for the first time in what seemed like forever.

"Cats or dogs?"

"Dogs—definitely dogs."

"Me too." He grinned. "Tea or coffee?"

"Coffee, baby." I laughed.

"Sweet or savory?"

"Ooh. That's a hard one. Depends on the day, but I like both, a lot." I laughed again.

"Cupcakes or cookies?"

"Cupcakes. You?"

"Cookies." He grinned. "I'm an enigma."

"Oh?"

"My favorite cookie is oatmeal raisin." He laughed. "My sister says I'm a weirdo."

"Oatmeal raisin cookies aren't bad." I grinned. "My favorite cupcakes are red velvet."

"I love red velvet cupcakes," he said and then he groaned. "Actually, I can't lie. I hate them. Just give me chocolate cupcakes without the food coloring."

"Haha," I laughed. "Not the same."

"I beg to differ." He grinned, his teeth white and shiny and slightly crooked, which gave him an even more endearing look.

"Sure, you do." I winked at him. "Any more questions?"

"Favorite movie?"

"Ooh, good one. Let me think. Uhm, I think it would have to be *Casablanca*."

"Oh, wow." He looked at me with an impressed expression. "I have to go with *The Godfather*. Favorite TV show?"

"Honestly?" I laughed. "I absolutely love *King of Queens*, because I think Kevin James is hilarious. You?"

"*Breaking Bad*, all day, every day." He grinned. "With *The Walking Dead* a close second."

"Aww, I haven't watched those shows yet," I said. "I need to, though."

"Maybe we can do a *Breaking Bad* marathon," he suggested. "I'd love to watch it all the way through again."

"Yeah, that would be cool," I agreed. "I've heard good things about it."

"Awesome." He broke off a piece of the muffin and continued chewing. "So there's this art exhibit coming to town next week featuring some impressionist pieces from Monet, Manet, Degas and some others from some private collection. I was wondering if you'd be interested in going with me?"

"Are you asking me on a second date?" I asked, surprised.

"I know. I know. I should play it cooler." He laughed as he stared at me. "And I know you barely know me and this date has barely started, but I just wanted you to know that I'm definitely interested in seeing you again."

"Thank you. I think I'd like that." I nodded and took a piece of the muffin. "Now, tell me more about this movie that we're going to see. You've got me all curious."

"I can't tell you too much or I'll spoil it." He grinned. "But I can tell you that what you think is happening is not what's really happening or what's going to happen."

"Hmm, really?" I was thoughtful. "How so?"

"I can't tell you more." He laughed. "You'll just have to see."

"Argh. I hate surprises." I laughed, and then froze as I heard my phone beeping. I ignored the sound and tried to quiet the thought that perhaps it was Cody texting me. I was not going to think about him. I wanted him off of my mind.

"Is that your phone?" Luke asked me curiously. "I don't mind if you check your messages."

"No, it's fine. I'm sure it's nothing important." I smiled at him, ignoring the slight turning in my stomach.

"If you're sure," he said as he took another bite of the muffin. "Maybe your friends are texting you to make sure you're still alive. Or maybe they're trying to give you an out. Which I suppose is a good sign for me because you're not answering the phone and accepting it."

"This is a good date. I don't need to flee." I grinned and then frowned slightly as I heard my phone beeping again.

"Check it." He laughed. "Obviously whoever is trying to text you is concerned and needs an update."

"Haha, yeah, maybe," I said, my stomach churning as I picked up my phone. I put in my password and looked at my messages. There was a message from Mila and several from Cody. I took a deep breath and opened up the messages. *Sally, I'm so sorry about what happened this afternoon. Please forgive me. Have a nice date. I'm sure he'll love you. You're an awesome gal. Please call me when you get back from your date so I know everything is okay.* I stared at the screen, my heart once again feeling low. I felt a burning pain and anger at Cody as I stared at his messages. Why couldn't he just leave me alone? Why did he have to torment me so? I looked up at Luke, who was staring at me curiously, and I gave him a weak smile. "It's my friend Mila making sure the date is going well." I looked back down at my phone and deleted the messages from Cody. I wasn't going to respond. And I sure as hell wasn't going to call him later. He could piss off. I was done with him. I wasn't playing his games any longer. I didn't need any more heartache and I didn't want to waste my time anymore.

"So tell me more about this movie, then," I said to Luke as I put my phone back into my bag. "What exactly did your friend work on?" I leaned forward and pushed Cody to the back of my mind. I was going to focus on Luke now. He seemed nice and cute and he was interested in me, which was a great thing. I needed someone who wanted to see me and hang out with me, not someone who wanted to play games with my heart.

CHAPTER FIFTEEN

Cody

"So how was your third date with, Luke?" Mila asked Sally, and I felt my stomach curdle involuntarily. I looked at Sally's face, a grin plastered on mine, but inside I wasn't feeling like smiling. I watched as Sally giggled nervously and, as her eyes looked into mine, I could see a flush on her face. I could tell she'd had fun and that made me mad. Not that it was the only reason why I was feeling pissed. Sally hadn't responded to any of my texts or Facebook messages since the day we'd made love, and it was driving me crazy not knowing what she was thinking or doing. Or how her date with Luke had gone. Now I knew it had gone well, seeing as Mila was talking about three dates. Three dates in two weeks? What the hell? Was the guy eager or what? I could feel my stomach churning as I wondered if they'd kissed or made love. Was that why she hadn't messaged me back? Had she already moved on? I sat there trying to pretend I didn't want to ask Mila to leave the room. I was lucky to even have gotten an invite to hang out, seeing as it seemed like Sally was trying to avoid me.

"It was fun, thanks," she said simply, her eyes on Mila. She still had barely looked at me and it was infuriating. Was she going to continue ignoring me?

"What did you guys do? Did he kiss you yet?" Mila asked

eagerly, and I wanted to tell her to shut up. I didn't want to hear about Sally's date. Who cared? I guessed the feeling in my stomach told me that some part of me cared. And that made me mad. I didn't care about the dates. I more cared that she was upset at me. Sally wasn't what I wanted. She was a great girl, but I didn't love her and I didn't want to spend my life with her. To be fair, I couldn't see myself spending my life with anyone. I ignored the voice in me that was telling me I was lying to myself. I just couldn't let myself get into this situation. I wasn't sure what I was thinking or feeling anymore. I just knew I was starting to feel like I was going crazy and that I couldn't get Sally out of my mind and I just wasn't sure why. *I should be happy she's dating someone she likes. I should be happy that she's finding love, because I sure as hell can't give her that.* We just weren't compatible in that regard. And to pretend otherwise just wasn't fair. It wasn't fair to her, and Mila would kill me if I continued to push things knowing that. I could ignore the small pangs of annoyance and pain that befell me when Sally talked about men. I would just have to get over it. I mean, she deserved a good guy. Deserved a man who wanted what she wanted. In truth, I was still attracted to other women, even though I was also attracted to Sally.

But even though I knew her style of commitment wasn't for me, there were times I looked at Sally and my heart skipped not one but two beats. Sometimes, I didn't want to walk away from her. Sometimes, I could just drown in her eyes. Sometimes, I just wanted to reach out and touch her cheek or brush a hair away from her face. Sometimes, I just wanted to hold her hand. When her face looked sad or when I heard uncertainty in her voice, I just wanted to tell her she could talk to me. I wanted to tell her there was nothing she couldn't share with me. And more recently, I hadn't been able to sleep without thinking of her and checking her Facebook page to see if I could find out what she was doing. I checked my phone umpteen times a day to see if she'd texted me back. I wanted to know what she was thinking, if she was mad. I had knots in my stomach. And I hated it. I hated this feeling of uncertainty. I hated not knowing why I felt this way. I hated thinking about her with Luke.

I wanted her here with me. I wanted to talk to her. I wanted us to laugh together. I wanted everything to be normal again. If I was honest, I certainly didn't want to hear about Luke. I didn't want to hear about her laughing, thinking, feeling, touching another guy. I didn't analyze why I didn't want to hear about it. It didn't matter. It was probably a gut reaction, some sort of alpha chemical bullshit that made me feel things I didn't really feel. I just had to keep reminding myself of that fact. I did not love Sally. I did not want to date Sally. We were not compatible. A relationship between the two of us would never work. It would never be anything more than sex for me and she was ultimately worth more than that. She was a good person. She deserved the best. She deserved a real love. She deserved to have the best part of someone. And I couldn't allow my temporary jealousy to ruin that for her. I had to not be selfish. I had to be a good friend. I had to show her I could be a good friend. I needed her to forgive me. I needed to be back in her life. I needed her to give me that smile she only gave me. That feeling that warmed me inside. She'd make a good girlfriend. I knew that. She needed someone who could give her back that same devotion.

Sometimes I wished I could be that man, the one who could give her that. Sometimes I thought perhaps I could be that man. On good days when the sun was shining and everything was right in my world, I thought I could be her knight in shining armor. I thought maybe I should ignore the inner voice and just go with my feelings, but then I thought to myself, what would I say? What would I do? What did I really feel? I knew I didn't really appreciate the feelings she made me feel inside. They made me uncomfortable. And I wasn't sure if the feelings she made me feel inside were due to her ignoring me. What if everything went back to normal and I didn't care so much anymore?

Everything about this situation made me uncomfortable, and while sometimes I appreciated being taken out of my comfort zone, for the most part I didn't. I didn't like the way she made me feel. I didn't like the ups and downs of being around her. I liked to be even-keeled. I liked just feeling good, and she didn't always make me feel good. I couldn't explain it. I'd never had someone make me feel so happy from just laughing at my jokes. It was a weird experience. To feel. To be so influenced by someone else's reactions to me. I didn't know why I cared. It was just Sally. And yet, here I sat, wondering what she was thinking and feeling and when she'd look at me and give me that smile that would let me know everything between us was okay again.

"So, what do you think, Cody?" Mila asked me, and I looked up in confusion.

"Think about what?" I blinked. I could see Sally's eyes on me, a weird expression on her face as they both gazed at me.

"What Luke said to Sally." Mila sighed in annoyance. "Do you think that means he's into her or do you think he's just playing with her? I mean, I think it's fairly obvious he's into her."

"Sorry, what?" I blinked, annoyed that the Luke conversation was still going on, even though I had obviously spaced out. Why couldn't girls talk about anything other than guys?

"Do you think Luke likes Sally?" Mila asked again, spacing out her words slowly, enunciating each syllable exaggeratingly.

"How the fuck am I supposed to know?" I said, letting my frustrations out as I replied. I could see Sally's eyes widening as

Mila glared at me.

"You're such an asshole, Cody. If you'd been listening to what I'd just been saying instead of daydreaming about heaven-knows-what…"

"Shut up, Mila." I glared at her. Then I looked over at Sally. "Look, if he asks you out again, that's a pretty good indication he likes you." I paused and cleared my throat. "Unless of course you have already had sex with him." I stared her down, trying to see if I could tell from her reaction if she'd slept with him. My body felt tense as I tried to figure it out.

"Cody!" Mila shouted at me. "What are you trying to say?"

"I'm just saying that if Sally already gave the milk away for free, he may not be interested in buying the cow."

"You're such an asshole." Mila looked at me with such a venomous glare that I almost burst out laughing.

"What? You wanted a guy's perspective, right?" I glared back at her. "Isn't that why I'm here and TJ was smart enough to have alternate plans?" I raised an eyebrow at the two women, not even caring that I was being deliberately offensive and annoying. Had she slept with him or not?

"TJ had to work, something you rarely do," Mila responded. "And you didn't come to dish out any guy advice, you came for free food, so stop acting like you're some sort of god or hero or advice-uncle because we asked you one question. You didn't even listen to what we were saying, so you officially suck in that role anyway."

"Fine!" I put my hands up and sighed. "I'm listening. Tell me the story. What the fuck did Frank say to Sally that has her knickers in a twist?" I didn't even try to hide my annoyance.

"His name is Luke." Mila rolled her eyes.

"And my knickers aren't in a twist," Sally responded, her face looking slightly bewildered, though I don't know why she was confused. She'd been around Mila and me arguing for years. This was nothing new. Unless of course she had reason to believe she knew why I was so agitated. Something in me froze as I thought about her realizing there was more going on here. Was she realizing that perhaps I had feelings for her? I shook my head slightly at the thought. How could she know? I didn't even know what sort of feelings I had for her. And if anything, she was bewildered by the fact that I was even sitting here, listening to their girl-talk in the first place.

"Just tell me the story again." I rolled my eyes impatiently. "What did Frank—I mean, Luke—say that has you wondering if he's a good guy or not?"

"I don't know if I should bother repeating the story now," Mila said with a glare.

"Why are you telling the story?" I gave her a look. "Isn't this something happening in Sally's life? Shouldn't she be the one asking me?"

"Are you saying that's the reason why you weren't listening in the first place?" Mila rolled her eyes. "Because I was telling the story, as opposed to Sally?"

"That's exactly why." I nodded sternly. "Who can take you seriously, Mila?" I looked over at Sally. "I'm listening. Feel free to go ahead."

"Uhm, it's okay." Sally looked at me awkwardly and I just wanted to take her into my arms and kiss her and tell her to forget Luke.

"Sally, just tell me. After all this, I really want to know," I muttered, feeling frustrated.

"So sincere, Cody." Mila rolled her eyes and stood up. "I'm going to get another bottle of wine. Does anyone want anything?"

"Some chips and dip," I hollered. "And some beers. I don't

want wine."

"How am I supposed to carry wine, beer, chips and dip?" Mila looked at me. "Do you see a third and fourth arm connected to my body?"

"I wouldn't be shocked, since you are deformed-looking." I laughed at Mila's glare. "But no, you can do what all regular humans do in these situations."

"What's that?" She had such a curious expression on her face that I had to stop myself from calling her a dumbass. What did she think I was going to say? How many different solutions did she see to this problem?

"What's it worth to you?" I asked her with a grin.

"Cody! It's not worth anything." She glared. "Just tell me."

"Okay, well…" I paused for dramatic effect and laughed at the anticipatory looks on Mila's and Sally's faces.

"Just say it," Mila groaned, and I put my hands in the air.

"Well, the secret to carrying it all back…" I said, pausing some again before continuing, "is to take two trips."

"Two trips," Mila repeated after me, dumfounded, as if not fully comprehending what I'd said. "You're an asshole, Cody." She shook her head, and I laughed and gave Sally a look. Sally was trying not to laugh, and I gave her a small wink as our eyes met. She started laughing then and a small rush of warmth spread through me at her laughter. My heart expanded for a few seconds as I looked at her and I wondered momentarily if this was what love felt like. What would it be like to feel this light-hearted happiness on a daily basis? Was that even possible?

"I guess you can start telling him the story as I go and work as the scullery maid," Mila said as she left the room.

"So…?" I looked at Sally with a soft smile, trying to ignore the bitter feelings that were starting to emerge as I waited for her to tell me about the dick she was dating.

"I don't have to say anything." She shook her head and I could see that she was embarrassed. "It's really not much."

"Look, I don't mind," I said too roughly, so I made a big scene of clearing my throat so that she would think that the reason I sounded annoyed was more related to being sick as opposed to being extremely annoyed.

"Well, if you're sure," she said uncertainly.

"So go ahead, spill it," I said, trying not to grit my teeth and ask her instead why she hadn't returned my texts or messages.

"So Luke and I went out last night," she said hesitantly, and it took everything in me to not tell her to just get on with it. I didn't want to hear her story. I didn't want to know anything about Luke. I didn't want to hear her story at all. I didn't care if she never saw him again. I didn't care if I never heard about him again. He could drop off a cliff and die for all I cared.

"Continue." I nodded, keeping all my other thoughts inside.

"So everything seemed to be going well," she continued softly. "We had a lot of good eye-contact, which is a good thing, right?"

"Yeah." I nodded. *If he wants to get in your pants*, I said inside.

"So we were joking around and I thought everything was going really well." She paused and I watched as she nibbled on her lower lip. I stared at her lush pink lips for a few seconds and tried just to think about how they would feel on me, sucking. I felt myself growing hard at the thought. What would she do if I reached over and pulled her on top of me? Would she let me take her again? Did she want that as well? Maybe that would make her forget Luke. Maybe that was what I needed to get over the craziness in my head again. Maybe I needed to have her again. She was still in my blood and I hadn't had my fill of her. I wanted to touch her, feel her, wanted to be inside of her.

"Yeah, continue," I said, trying to distract myself from where my thoughts were going. I wasn't going to be able to stop myself from getting carried away if I kept thinking about making love to her. And I knew the last thing I needed to be doing was trying to seduce her again.

"Well, it was weird," she said. "The mood just really changed at one point and I don't know why."

"What do you mean the mood changed?" I asked her, genuinely curious. Was it over between her and Luke already? I couldn't help feeling smug and happy inside at that thought.

"Well, the smile left his face and he started talking about how he had to go home," she said softly.

"Oh?" I gazed at her. "What happened right before that?" Yup, it was over! I wondered if it would be too much if I asked her to come over to my place to watch a movie?

"Honestly, I don't know." She shrugged. "Nothing. I don't remember anything happening. We were just talking. I didn't say anything untoward, I don't think."

"Hmm, that doesn't make much sense, though. Something had to have been said for his mood to change." I pretended like I still cared about the conversation while I thought about sliding inside of her from behind. I wondered if she liked doggy-style. Who was I kidding? What woman didn't like doggy-style?

"The conversation was fine, I thought." She sighed and I could see a hurt and confused expression in her eyes. "We were just talking and then I got a text message."

"Ooh, did you check your messages during the date?" I asked her. "That might have pissed him off." I wondered who had texted her? Was it another guy? I frowned. Was she talking to more than one guy online?

"I didn't check anything." She shook her head. "I didn't want to be rude, so I didn't check."

"Okay." I frowned. So maybe she was really into this guy if she wasn't even checking her messages on the date. For some reason, this displeased me even more and I tried to shake the feeling off. I couldn't believe my mood was going up and down with the conversation. What was wrong with me? Was I becoming a girl?

"Yeah, I hate when guys are on their phones on dates, so I never do it," she said softly.

"Yeah, that's rude. A clear sign of disinterest," I said, as I gazed at her fingers in her lap, remembering when they'd been on me, touching me and teasing me.

"Yeah." She nodded in agreement. "But yeah, he wasn't on his phone and I wasn't on mine. Though we both heard my phone beeping a couple of times."

"Hmm, okay, and that's when everything changed?" I said, though I didn't really want to continue the conversation.

"Yeah." She nodded "And then basically at the end of the date, he told me he had to go and run some errands, but earlier he said that he wanted to take me to get ice cream."

"Hmm, that's weird." I gave her a look. "So something turned him off."

"Yeah, I mean, I didn't ask him about the ice cream again. I figured if he wanted to extend the date he would have brought it up, since he already knew that I was down for it."

"So then what happened?"

"Well, then he paid, walked me to my car and left." She made a face.

"And left?"

"Yup—no kiss, no hug, no nothing, not even eye-contact, really."

"That's weird." Had they kissed before? Jealousy stirred in my stomach. Had her tongue been in his mouth? Had he touched her? I felt my hands curling into fists at the thought.

"Yup." She nodded. "I just don't understand."

"And the date started well?"

"I thought it was going fantastically." She made a face. "But maybe I have absolutely no clue."

"Well, no, I'm sure you do. Maybe he got the vibe that you weren't into him or maybe he realized that you're a good girl and you weren't going to sleep with him, which actually would make a lot of sense, because maybe that's why he chose to forgo the ice cream. Maybe he was thinking the ice cream would be used for something else later that night. Maybe he had no plans to actually *eat* the ice cream."

"What are you talking about?" Sally looked confused.

"I mean, maybe the ice cream was going to be used in the bedroom for a different sort of dessert."

"Oh?" Sally mouthed the word, looking at me with wide eyes. I felt a surge of happiness at her response. They obviously had not slept together if this was her response to my ice-cream comment. I wasn't sure why that made me so happy, but it did.

"Yeah, he probably was thinking ice cream, whipped cream, maybe some chocolate sauce, but all for the bedroom, and when he realized that wasn't happening, he was like, 'Forget this. Let me not waste another twenty bucks on this date'," I continued happily, my mind already thinking about licking whipped cream off of all of her private parts.

"Hmm." Sally pursed her lips. "I'm not sure." She made a face. "I don't think he's that kind of guy. He never made any comments like that on our previous dates."

"Trust me, I know what I'm saying. I'm a guy. I know how we are." *I want to lick ice cream off of you right now*, I thought to myself. *And you can suck it off of me too*, I thought, growing even harder.

"If you say so." She looked away from me for a few seconds and for some reason that made me angry. Was she thinking about him?

"Did you really like him or something?" I snapped at her.

"Huh?" She looked back at me and blinked.

"You seem to care an awful lot about what this guy said or did. Forget him. There are much better guys out there."

"I didn't say I cared. I'm just confused."

"No need to be confused. I just explained it all to you in a nutshell."

"Okay. Thanks." She nodded just as Mila walked back into the room with a bottle of wine and a bag of chips.

"Thanks for what?" Mila looked at me. "What advice did you give her?"

"I told her he just wanted sex and that was why he peaced-out."

"Cody, are you for real?" Mila sighed. "Why would you say that?"

"Because I know guys." I shrugged. "You wanted me to give my honest opinion, right?" I looked at them both. "The dude realized he wasn't going to get laid so he peaced-out. It happens all the time."

"I don't think Luke is like that." Sally shook her head. "He doesn't seem to be about sex."

"Every guy is about sex." I was exasperated at how clueless Sally was being and how Mila was trying to make me out to be the bad guy. "Trust me, I'm a guy, I know these things."

"Every guy isn't you, Cody." Mila pursed her lips. "I'm sure there's a perfectly good explanation as to why Luke left."

"Okay, so why ask me, then?" I rolled my eyes and I could feel myself growing angry. Why was I wasting my time here in this situation? I was getting absolutely nothing from it. This wasn't what I'd come for. This wasn't what I wanted.

"We thought you could give us a male perspective. Well, I thought that." Mila sighed. "Sally didn't really know you were coming."

"I see." I looked over at Sally then and watched her face and waited for her to look at me. "I texted you," I said nonchalantly, like it wasn't a big deal that I'd texted her several times and she hadn't responded. Over ten times to be exact.

"Oh?" She looked up at me with a surprised expression.

"Is your phone broken?" I felt some sudden hope. Maybe that was why she hadn't texted?

"Nope, why?" she answered quickly and then her face flushed as she realized why I'd asked her the question.

"No reason." I shook my head. "I suppose you didn't forget your Facebook password either?" I said with a smile, though my stomach was churning.

"I've just been busy."

"With Luke? I know." I looked away from her and I could see Mila looking at me curiously, studying my face, and I stared back at her, wondering what she was thinking.

"I'm going to the bathroom. I'll be back," Mila said abruptly and left the room. I stared at the door for a few seconds and then looked towards Sally.

"So how have you been?" I asked her quietly.

"Good," she said simply.

"That's good," I replied. "I've been pretty good too."

"That's nice." She nodded and I could tell that she wasn't even engaged in our conversation.

"I'm sorry." I stood up and walked over to her and crouched down next to her. "You know that, right?"

"There's nothing to be sorry about." She shrugged and looked at me.

"Sally…" I grabbed her hand and she flinched away from me. "Sally," I said, a little bit more harshly, hurt at her reaction. "Can we please talk?"

"Talk about what, Cody?" She sighed and glanced at me. "If it's about the sex, it's fine. We both enjoyed it. I'm over it. I'm not even thinking about it anymore, okay? I'm meeting new guys. I'm dating. I'm focusing on that."

"Okay." I frowned at her tone. If she was okay, why wasn't she acting like she normally did? "You haven't texted or messaged me back, so I figured something was up."

"Like I said, I've been busy."

"Too busy to text me back?" I said softly and I touched her face lightly. "Look at me, please, Sally."

"What do you want me to say, Cody?" She sighed and looked into my eyes. "I'm not sure what you want me to say. You're confusing me."

"I'm confusing you?" I stared back at her. "How am I confusing you? You're the one not responding to my texts."

"I just can't do this." She sighed. "Look, it doesn't matter, does it? Are you really that upset because I didn't send you a couple of texts back?"

"It's rude," I said with a frown, my heart pounding. "And I was worried about you."

"Then, sorry." She stood up abruptly. "I'll be better."

"Sally, what's going on?" I asked her, feeling frustrated and upset. "Why are you being this way?"

"I'm not being any way. I'm just tired." She closed her eyes and sighed deeply before looking at me again.

"I've missed you," I said sincerely, not knowing why I was telling her that. "I've missed hanging out with you and talking to you and spending time with you."

"Thanks," she said and gave me a weak smile.

"I know you don't or won't believe me, but I value your presence in my life." I felt empty inside as I stared at her. "I miss being with you."

"Okay."

"I'm sorry about what I said about Luke." I made a face. "Maybe I'm wrong." I sighed. "Maybe I just said that because I wanted you to go off him. Maybe I'm jealous that you're seeing someone." The words tripped out of my mouth uncomfortably and we both just stood there and stared at each other for a few seconds. "Say something, Sally."

"I don't know what to say, Cody." She sounded exasperated. "What do you want me to say? Do you want me to tell you that I like you? Is that what you want to hear?"

"You like me?" My heart raced at her words and I grinned at her.

"Don't act like you didn't know." She rolled her eyes at me, but I could see her face flushing as she tried to read me. "This is hard for me, Cody. You're confusing me. You're so hot and cold, and I just don't know what you want from me. What you think of me, you know? I just don't understand you."

"I don't understand me sometimes, either." I flashed her a small smile. "Come back with me to my place," I asked her softly. "We can talk." I walked toward her. "I want us to be on the same page. I don't want you to think I'm being hot and cold. I like you as well, Sally," I said and I felt like a huge weight had been lifted off my chest. "I really do like you. I've been thinking about you a lot recently." I paused, not knowing what else to say. I wasn't comfortable talking about feelings and I honestly didn't really know what I felt. I knew I'd been unhappy. I knew I missed her. I knew I'd felt guilty. I knew I wanted her in my life. But aside from that, I didn't know what I wanted. I didn't want to lie to her. I didn't want to tell her things that weren't true just because I thought she'd want to hear them. I didn't know what to say because I didn't really know how I felt.

"I don't know if that's a good idea, Cody." She stumbled over her words hesitantly and I knew she wasn't sure if she should come over.

"Please," I asked her softly. "Just come over and let's really talk and get over everything. I want everything to be normal between us again. We can watch a movie and eat ice cream. I know you love that."

"You don't want to watch a movie and eat ice cream," she said with a smile.

"With you, I do," I said with a nod. And I was being honest. I'd do anything in this moment just to be with her and make everything right in the world. I needed everything to go back to the way it was. I needed her to be okay with me. I needed to feel normal inside. I was fed up with the anxiety and angst. That wasn't who I was. That wasn't who I wanted to be. I didn't want to feel this way. And I knew the only way to get rid of it was for Sally to forgive me so we could move on with our friendship and continue as we were. That's all I wanted and needed.

"Okay," she said uncertainly. "I'll come and watch a movie with you, if you let me choose the movie."

"Oh, God, you're going to pick a chick-flick, aren't you?" I groaned, and she laughed.

"Hey, you're the one who wants me to come over."

"Fine." I made a face. "Just nothing too icky."

"We'll see," she said light-heartedly, and I felt my stomach settling slightly. Things were starting to get back to normal. She was laughing with me and looking me in the eyes. I could tell that her icy exterior was melting and she was warming to me once again. Everything in my world would be back to normal soon.

"*BRIDGET JONES'S DIARY?* Really?" I groaned as I leaned back on the couch and stared at the TV screen. "That's what we're watching?"

"Hey, you're lucky I'm here watching anything with you." Sally shook her head and giggled slightly. "Mila thinks I'm crazy and I think I'm crazy, so you should thank your lucky stars."

"You're not crazy." I laughed. "At least not crazier than any other girl."

"Why thanks, don't I feel special." Sally pouted at me and I leaned over to tickle her.

"You should feel special. You should feel very special," I said as she giggled and pulled away from me.

"Cody, stop it." She squealed as I continued to make her squirm.

"Why?" I asked her softly, my face close to hers as I continued to tickle her under the arms, enjoying being close to her.

"Because we're meant to be watching this movie," she said between laughs, her eyes bright as she gazed at me.

"You watch and I tickle. Seems like a fair deal," I said, my face close to hers now. "Right?"

"No." She shook her head as she gazed back at me. I stared at her lips and I knew what I wanted to do, though I was trying to stop myself from doing it.

"Why no?" I said as I leaned in closer, my lips a mere inch from hers.

"Cody, what are you doing?" she asked breathlessly, her eyes widening.

"Saying sorry," I said before leaning in to kiss her. Her lips were slightly parted as mine met hers and they tasted sweet as I pressed mine against hers. I felt my body sinking into hers, melding into her in a way that felt so right. My tongue entered her mouth quickly and I pushed her back against the couch so that I could adjust my position. Sally kissed me back eagerly and I felt her tongue against mine as her hands fell to my shoulders. We kissed deeply, passionately, wantonly, and my hands fell to her breasts and ran over them gently. Our breathing was heavy and I didn't want to pull away, but I knew I had to before I had her clothes off and she was naked on my couch.

"I hope my apology sufficed," I said as I pulled away from her reluctantly a few seconds later.

"It did," she squeaked out and licked her lips. She stared at me for a few seconds and then groaned. "What am I doing?" She shook her head, and I frowned.

"What are you talking about?" I could feel myself getting annoyed again. Was she mad that I'd kissed her? That she'd kissed me back?

"I just...I don't know." She bit down on her lower lip. "I'm not sure it was a good idea for me to come over and then to let you kiss me." She sighed. "I just don't know what I'm doing."

"You're hanging out with me and we're having a fun, relaxing time," I said and leaned back, pulling her into my arms. "Is there anything wrong with that?"

"No, yes—I don't know." She settled her head on my shoulder and sighed. "Why is this so hard?"

"I don't know why I'm hard," I joked. "Maybe because you're here with me."

"Cody!" She looked at me with an angry face for a few seconds and I froze, wondering if I'd gone too far. Had I pushed my luck? Why had I let myself get too comfortable around her again so easily? I wasn't sure why I always felt the need to touch her and have my hands on her, but I just needed to feel that connection with her. My body craved hers and not just in a sexual way. It just wanted to be close to her. I just wanted to be close to her. I wasn't sure what it was, but I was going to be really pissed with myself if I'd ruined the moment already.

"Sorry?" I gave her my most innocent, sweet-boy face and she laughed.

"You're not sorry." She gave me a beguiling look, her face radiating happiness, and I laughed along with her, everything suddenly right in my world again. "And I don't know if I want you to be sorry."

"You enjoy my kisses," I teased her, and she blushed. "Don't worry, I enjoy your kisses as well."

"You're the most confusing man I've ever met in my life, Cody." She shook her head. "You drive me crazy."

"In a good way, I hope."

"I don't know." She shook her head. "Is there a good kind of crazy?"

"It depends."

"On what?" she asked with a curious smile, and I let my fingers play with her hair.

"How good the sex is." I started chuckling. "If the girl can rock my world, then she can be a little crazy. If she's not doing much for me, she'd better be sane as hell."

"Cody, that's horrible." She shook her head and twisted her body around to look at me. She folded her legs up onto the couch and poked me in the chest. "You're really, really a bad guy—you know that, right?"

"Nah, I'm not," I said and grabbed her fingers and held them. "I'm really not."

"You are." She smiled at me. "You really are."

"I like to think I'm just honest."

"We all like to think we're honest. That doesn't mean we can say whatever crap we want to and think we're not going to offend anyone."

"I'm not trying to offend anyone," I said, then I looked at her for a few seconds. "Is that why you ignored me for the last couple of weeks? Did I offend you?"

"Cody." She rolled her eyes at me. "I already told you I wasn't ignoring you."

"Liar," I said to her, my eyes boring into hers with a challenge. "You were totally ignoring me."

"I wasn't. Would I be here if I was?"

"I don't know. Maybe? Maybe you couldn't resist me after seeing me at Mila's today," I joked, but I could see something in her expression changing. I felt warning bells in my ears and I knew I needed to change the subject again swiftly before I brought the mood down. "So, what have you been doing with yourself since I last saw you?"

"Not much." She shrugged. "Working. Dating."

"Ugh, I don't need to hear about loser-Luke again."

"He's not a loser." She shook her head at me and smiled slightly. I wanted to tell her that, yes, he was a loser, or at least the loser. He was a loser because she was here with me right now, letting me kiss her and touch her and he was somewhere in his bedroom or bathroom wondering where he went wrong.

"Anyway...next. What else? Any good gossip?"

"What good gossip would I have?" She giggled. "Nothing much is going on with me."

"Aww." I gave her a rueful look, but inside I was happy. Nothing much going on meant she wasn't doing much, which meant maybe she'd been thinking about me too, at least a little bit.

"Aww, nothing." She laughed. "What about you? What have you been up to?"

"Oh, not that much. A few dates." I almost groaned out loud

as the words slipped out of my mouth. *SHUT IT, Cody,* I screamed inside.

"Just a few?" Sally teased me, though I couldn't tell if she was masking her hurt. I'd spoken to TJ a few days before and he'd called me a fool for talking to Sally about other women. Even if I thought of her as just a friend, or a friend with benefits, or a special friend with benefits. He said he knew I wasn't looking to get married, but that it was insensitive of me to think I could be with Sally and talk to her about other girls; especially because we'd been intimate now. I'd been annoyed at his words, but I knew he was correct. We were past the 'just friends' stage now. And even though I'd gone on a few dates, all I'd been able to think about was Sally.

"Haha, they weren't really dates," I lied, trying to backtrack.

"What were they, then?" She looked at me curiously and I could see that her eyes were more intense than normal.

"Nothing," I said softly, not knowing what to say, how to get her to understand that I was in an awkward space. I was feeling things I didn't really comprehend or want to comprehend. She was making me feel things, and I didn't know how to define what we had. I didn't want to define it. I didn't want anything to change between us. I didn't want to let her go.

"Nothing?" Her expression looked sad suddenly and I pulled her onto my lap.

"I like you," I whispered in her ear. "I like you and I just want to focus on that, if that's okay?" My hand slid down her body and to the sweet spot between her legs and rubbed gently. She moaned slightly and looked me directly in the eyes. I could see a million thoughts crossing through her mind as she stared at me and I couldn't read a one of them. I waited with bated breath for her to respond. What was she thinking? What was going through her head? I just wanted to know. I wanted to know how she felt. What she wanted. Yet I didn't want to know. Not really. Knowing could ruin everything, and I couldn't stand for her to be out of my life again.

"I want to make love to you, Sally. Slowly. Quickly. Deeply. Forcefully. Teasingly." I leaned forward and nibbled on her earlobe as I continued to rub her. She shifted on my lap back and forth and I knew she was getting as excited as I was. "I want to make you mine. In all ways possible. I want to take you on the couch. In my bed. In the shower. On the kitchen counter. On the rug. On the balcony. I want you on your knees. On your back. Riding me. On my face. I want all of you. I want you. I want to drive you as crazy as you've made me. What do you say?" I paused then and waited. Waited for the answer that could either make or break this moment.

CHAPTER SIXTEEN

Sally

THAT MOMENT. THAT moment when time seems to stand still. That moment when all you can think about is him. That moment when all he can think about is you. That moment when he touches you. That moment when you touch him back. That moment when you cross the line. That moment when he is the only thing stopping you from losing control. That moment. That's the moment. That's the moment when you both go crazy. That's the moment where you lose yourself in everything you knew you should stay away from. This was the moment. This was the moment that shouldn't be happening. Not again, but I couldn't say no. I couldn't walk away.

"I didn't realize you were such a dirty talker," I said finally as Cody continued to rub me between the legs, turning me on and making my mind become mush. Why could I not focus on all the reasons why this was a bad idea? Was I that easy? Did I have no self-control? I thought about Luke for a second and about how I'd thought he was a nice guy until our last date when he'd just left. Maybe Cody was right. Maybe all Luke wanted was sex and he'd just been pretending to be a nice guy who was into me. I didn't know what Cody wanted from me, but at least now I knew he really was attracted to me and I knew he'd been jealous, or at least kind of jealous. And that, well, that made me feel amazing. It was pitiful and sad, and I knew I was playing with fire, but I didn't even care.

"Do you like the dirty talk?" Cody asked as he leaned forward and kissed me. "Do you want me to tell you how I want to be inside of you right now?" he mumbled against my lips. "Do you want to know how bad I want to rip your jeans off and your panties and feel your wetness on my fingers, my tongue, my lips? How I want my cock to make you come as soon as I penetrate you?" He paused and then groaned as he grabbed my hand. "You can feel it now. He's throbbing, waiting for you to respond." He placed my hand on his member and it felt hard beneath my touch. I swallowed and gazed into his eyes. They were full of desire and lust and I knew that I couldn't say no. I didn't want to say no.

"Take your jeans off," I said, and before I knew what I was doing I was standing up and kneeling before him on the couch. I reached up to his zipper and button and undid the button before unzipping his jeans and pulling them down. He looked at me with a steady face and then started grinning as I reached up and pulled his briefs down as well, exposing his hardness to the air.

"You don't have to..." he started but his voice drifted off as I bent down and took him into my mouth. I loved the salty, warm taste of him as I felt him growing every time I moved my head up and down. He grabbed the top of my head and I could feel his body moving back and forth as I pleasured him, the guttural noises from his chest turning me on even more. "Sally," he grunted as he pulled my arms and stopped me. "It's my turn." He grinned as I looked up at him.

"But..." I started to talk, but he shook his head. I stared at him in confusion as I knew he'd been about to come soon.

"I want to pleasure you first." He lifted my arms up and pulled my top off quickly before undoing my bra. He then pulled his own shirt off and I undid my pants and slipped them off so that I was just standing there in my panties. "You are so sexy," he muttered as he gazed at my breasts and then leaned forward. "I want to slide your panties off and fuck you hard." He groaned as his hands reached over and played with my nipples.

"So why don't you?" I said softly, wanting to feel him inside of me once again.

"Because I'm already close to coming." His eyes were starry as he looked at me. "I want to take my time and pleasure you first. I need to wind down a bit before I enter you."

"I see." I grinned at him. "I guess I have that effect on you."

"The 'I can't think straight when I'm inside of you' effect?" He grinned. "Why, yes, you do."

"Good to know." I laughed, feeling heady and high. "What should I do with my power?"

"I don't know," he said as his fingers pinched my nipples a little harder and I cried out in pleasure and pain. "What should you do?" He leaned forward and took my right nipple into his mouth, nibbling and tugging with his teeth, so that all of my body was on fire and I could feel my panties growing wet.

"Cody," I moaned as I felt his fingers slipping into my panties and rubbing me again, only this time the feeling of his skin on mine was driving me even more crazy.

"Yes, Sally." His voice was deep and rough.

"I think I want you inside of me, right now." I moaned, not able to stop myself.

"Tell me again." He grunted, his hands moving faster.

"Cody." I let out a gasp as he pulled down my panties and fell back onto the couch, straddling me on his legs, so that I could feel his hardness right against my sweet spot.

"Take it, if you want it," he said, challenging me, a small smirk on his face as his hands moved to my ass and grabbed my ass-cheeks, moving me up and down on his hardness, so that I was grinding against him.

"Cody, please." I leaned forward and kissed the top of his chest and then bit down into his skin. He froze for a second at my bite and then started moving me even faster on him. I smiled as I felt him reach down and readjust himself against me. He was going to enter me and I was ready. Only, I didn't feel him thrusting inside of me. Instead, I felt the tip of him rubbing against me and I groaned.

"If you want it, come and get it," he whispered in my ear, and I looked up at him with a small smile before reaching down and slowly moving my body on top of him. I sat on his hardness then, easing him inside of me, and we both gasped with pleasure as I started moving back and forth, allowing and encouraging all of him deeper inside of me. I moved slowly at first, wanting to enjoy the feel of every inch of him, but Cody wasn't having that. I felt his hands on my hips as he bounced me up and down on him, and my breasts bounced back and forth against his chest as I rode him. I felt myself about to come when he suddenly stilled.

"Hold on." He groaned into my hair as he ran his hands down my back and then he moved me back and forth again quickly, groaning into my ear as I came against him, my body convulsing. "Oh, shit," he grunted as he lifted me off of him and pushed me back onto the couch. I felt his hardness on my stomach as he withdrew and the warm liquid of his pleasure splattered onto me.

"Sorry," he said as he grabbed his T-shirt from the floor and cleaned me up. "I thought that was better than inside of you."

"It was." I nodded and pulled him down on top of me. "But maybe we should remember protection next time."

"Maybe we should get you on birth control," he said with a small smile as he kissed me hard. "That way I can come inside of you and we don't have to worry about it."

"Well, you can come inside of me in a condom as well," I said, kissing him back, not believing we were having this conversation.

"That's not really inside of you. That's inside rubber," he whispered against my lips. "I want to be inside of you."

"Cody," I groaned as I felt his fingers rubbing me again. "You cannot be ready to go again? Can you?"

"That's a silly question." He laughed against my lips. "I told you I want to fuck you until you can't think about anything or anyone else, and that's what I'm going to do." He nibbled on my earlobe and I wrapped my legs around his waist. I could feel my body responding to him again, eager to be taken, but there was a voice inside of me that wasn't completely happy. There was a voice inside of me that was telling me that maybe I'd made a mistake. I'd come back to Cody's place because I'd thought he'd been jealous. And because he'd said he liked me. And he'd missed me. And I thought that perhaps his wanting to sleep with me meant something more. But what if all it was, was sex? What if that was all he really cared about? How many times was he going to tell me he wanted to fuck me? Was he ever going to be able to see past that? I could feel a piece of my heart aching as I felt him growing hard against me again. I loved being with him. Loved how he made me feel. Loved making love to him, but I wanted and needed more than this. Only a few weeks ago, I'd vowed to myself that I was going to move on from Cody. I'd vowed I wasn't going to succumb to his smiles and sweet-talk. I'd vowed that I needed to get over him, but here I was, under him. Once again, I'd fallen victim to his spell and I wasn't sure if I'd made a huge mistake or not.

I LAY IN Cody's bed, feeling slightly sleepy, slightly empowered and totally confused. I wasn't sure what to think or feel, and I also knew that now wasn't the time to try and have a conversation with Cody about what was going on between us. I closed my eyes and sighed to myself. I was in both the best and worst position of my life. I was finally close to Cody in an intimate way and yet, I was also far away from the actual relationship I wanted with him. I didn't even understand why he wasn't interested in a real relationship. It didn't really make sense to me, but I didn't really want to ask.

I closed my eyes and pulled the sheets up to my face and just lay there, enjoying my time alone in his bed, not thinking about what he was doing for once in my life. I knew what he was doing. He was downstairs watching football in his living room, allowing me to sleep because he'd worn me out. I sighed to myself as I realized that I'd rather he'd have stayed upstairs and cuddled me and talked about where our relationship was going, but I knew that was way too much to ask.

I grabbed my handbag and pulled my phone out and was surprised to see that I had ten missed messages from Luke. I immediately felt guilty at seeing his name on the screen. Not that I had any real reason to feel guilty. We weren't dating. I wasn't cheating on him. In fact, he'd been the one to leave me feeling confused. I opened the messages and read them quickly. My heart started pounding as I read them and I put my phone down on the bed quickly before reading them again.

Hey Sally, I want to apologize for the other night and leaving so abruptly. I know you might be confused and I know I still owe you ice cream. I want to explain myself and I don't want you to think I'm crazy. I really like you, yes I know this is early to say this. I really feel a strong connection to you and the other night I had an overwhelming urge to kiss you and touch you. I left because I didn't want you to think I was all about sex. I didn't want to be that guy who can't keep his hands off you. And I didn't know how to explain that without seeming like a weirdo. I'd really like to see where this goes. I know this is a really long text and I'd love to be able to see you and talk it all out in person, if you have time and still want to see me. Let me know!

I stared at my phone screen and I could feel my stomach churning. I bit down on my lower lip as I read his text yet another time. I was confused at the happy thoughts going through my head. I was happy that Luke had texted me and at what he'd said. A part of me was really happy, really excited. He had said all the words I'd wanted to hear from a guy. He valued and liked me. And he respected me enough to not just be all about my body. *Unlike Cody* flashed through my mind. Cody was all about the sex. He didn't seem to care that it was making a complicated situation even more complicated. He didn't care that we had this weird connection that we weren't really getting to the bottom of. Yeah, he'd said he liked me, but that was like the weakest thing he could have said in the situation. What did him liking me really mean? It was almost as if he'd said it just to get me into bed. Once I'd said yes, all other talk had been off the table.

I wanted to bang my head against a wall. I was so confused and frustrated with myself. And now I was even starting to doubt my feelings for Cody. If I loved him so much, how could I be so happy at Luke's text? How could I be feeling that maybe I should give Luke another chance? How could I be wondering if sleeping with Cody again had been the biggest mistake of my life? I knew that l loved him. I loved him so much that my heart hurt just thinking about not being with him, but I also knew that I liked Luke. Like, *really* liked him. I was attracted to him. He made me laugh. He made me smile. When I was with him, I rarely thought of Cody. A part of me knew that I could be happy with Luke. A part of me wondered if I could even love him if I let go of Cody, and that scared the shit out of the other part of me. I'd always lived my life with the philosophy that people had one true love, but if Cody wasn't the one, then maybe that wasn't true. I also knew that if I wanted to move on with Luke, I'd have to cut Cody off completely. I'd have to have him out of my life. I couldn't move on from him if I saw him and talked to him. I couldn't let go of him if I still had him in my soul. And the thought of never seeing him, not talking to him, never touching him again scared the shit out of me. It made me feel like I wanted to die. But the possibility of losing him, but gaining the opportunity to fly, always beckoned too brightly.

I didn't even know how to respond to Luke. I knew my response would signal something to him and I wasn't sure it was fair to make him believe I wanted the same thing if I was still committed to Cody. Also, I didn't know if it was right to enter a relationship with him to get over someone else? It all seemed so murky and the last thing I wanted to do was to hurt him. I liked him too much.

"Hey, you're up." Cody walked into the room and I jumped up in surprise as I hadn't even noticed him coming. I hadn't even heard him. My heart thudded in the way it always did when I saw him, unable to stop the love from flowing. I couldn't stop myself from lighting up.

"Yeah, how was the game?" I asked him softly, pushing my phone under my back.

"Still on, not sure who's going to win, so that's always a good game."

"Oh, cool." I nodded, not really sure what to say. I felt tongue-tied. And awkward.

"Not really." He smiled and walked to the bed. "Are you

hungry?"

"I'm okay, thanks." I shook my head.

"Sore?"

"A bit." I nodded and gave him a weak smile. Something felt off and I knew it was all inside of me, but I didn't know what to do about it. I just wanted to cry. I could feel it inside of me, welling up. I could feel the pain inside of me wanting to come out. I wanted to cry. I wanted to sob for the heartbreak and misery I still felt. I was maybe even more miserable than before because a part of me felt used and another part of me felt like I'd screwed myself over. Sleeping with Cody had brought him closer to my heart, but emotionally I felt like we were still nowhere. We were still nothing.

"Need anything?" he asked me softly as he sat down on the side of the bed and kissed me on the cheek.

"No, I'm okay, thanks." I pretended to yawn and then closed my eyes.

"Still tired?" he asked, surprised, and I nodded, not wanting to look at him. I didn't want to look into his piercing eyes. They did too much to me. Staring at his handsome face made me think things I didn't want to think. I was annoyed at myself for still hoping this could grow into something more than it was. Nothing Cody had said could really lead me to believe there was any possibility of him falling in love with me and us getting married and living happily ever after. Nothing Cody had said would lead me to believe he was really and truly my Prince Charming. Not now. Not after everything that had gone down between us. "Shall I try and wake you up?" I felt his lips against mine and I resisted kissing him back.

"No," I mumbled, annoyed. Could he only think about sex? Was this always just going to be a booty-call? Wasn't I worth more than that? Didn't I deserve more than that? I loved him, but I valued myself more than what he was offering. I thought about Luke and how sweet he was. I thought about his text message and how sincere he sounded, how he really wanted to get to know me. How he could possibly offer me what I really wanted. And ultimately that was what it was all about. It was about being with someone who could give me what I wanted. Love me in the way I wanted and deserved to be loved. I was fed up with the heartache. Love wasn't supposed to be this hard. Life wasn't supposed to be this hard.

I didn't want to be living on the edge of uncertainty forever.

"Sally, you okay?" Cody collapsed on the bed next to me and I could tell from his voice that he was feeling unsure of himself.

"I'm fine, why?" I opened my eyes and looked over at him. He was staring at my face and his eyes were narrowed as he gazed at me. "What's up?"

"What's up with you?" he asked me with a slight frown. "You're acting different."

"What do you mean?" I blinked at him, pretending I didn't understand what he was talking about.

"I mean, you can barely look me in the eyes right now." He reached over and touched my lips. "What's going on?"

"I'm just tired. I can barely keep my eyes open right now." I blinked again and yawned widely. "It's nothing personal."

"Are you still mad at me? Is that what this is all about?" He sighed.

"I'm not mad at you." I shook my head and reached over and touched his face, wanting so bad to tell him that I loved him, wanting so bad for him to know that all I wanted was to lie in his arms forever. I just wanted to be with him and hold him close. When I was around him I was no longer myself. I hated and loved the power he had over me.

"Why does it feel like you're mad at me, then?" he said as his hand grabbed mine and he brought my fingers to his lips for a kiss.

"I don't know." I shrugged. "You tell me."

"Sally, I don't know what's going on. I just know how I feel in this moment. I know something doesn't feel right. I know you're not acting how you normally act. I know something seems off."

"Wow, you know a lot," I answered with a small smile, trying to joke. "When did you get so smart?"

"We have a connection, Sally. I don't understand it and I've never been so attuned to someone else before, but I know something isn't right." He sighed. "But fine, you don't have to tell me."

"What connection do you think we have?" I asked softly, wanting him to continue. Maybe if he—if we—could talk this out, somehow we'd get to a place that felt better.

"I don't know." He sighed. "Maybe because we've known each other for so long and because we're better friends now, and now we're lovers, maybe I can just understand you better now. Maybe I can read your cues better now that you're in my life more. I don't really know why or how. Does it really matter?"

"I guess not." I sighed. "Why should it matter, right? Why does any of it matter? It's just nothing. It's all just nothing."

"What is that supposed to mean? It's just nothing?" He gave a deep sigh. "Why do I feel like we're fighting and I don't even know why?"

"If you don't know why, then it doesn't matter, right?" I pulled my hand away from his and sat up quickly. "I just can't do this anymore, Cody. I just don't have the strength to go back and forth with you all the time."

"Go back and forth about what?" He sat up as well and his voice was angry. "What the hell is going on, Sally? I thought we were in a good place? I thought everything was okay? Shit, we just made love five times."

"It always comes back to sex for you, doesn't it?" I put my hands on my face. "I want more than that."

"What?" He jumped off the bed and looked at me. "What the hell are you talking about? What do you mean it always comes back to sex for us? When has our relationship ever just been about sex?"

"What relationship?" I said and jumped up out of bed. "Do we have a relationship? Do we have anything?"

"What do you mean do we have a relationship?" He frowned. "Of course we do."

"What's our relationship, then?" I heard the words out loud and my whole body froze. I couldn't believe I was having this conversation here and now. I couldn't believe I was going for it. I knew I sounded crazy, like some sort of stalking obsessed person, but I couldn't keep doing this. I couldn't keep hoping and praying and falling back into this trap. He either wanted me or he didn't. I couldn't keep giving my body to him. I couldn't keep letting my heart have this hope and want. It wasn't fair, and I knew that every time it didn't go well, I was losing a part of myself. My soul was splintered and I didn't want to live this way anymore. My life and his love weren't worth all of this.

"I didn't know we had a defined relationship," he said slowly, his face going red. "We've never discussed anything like that."

"We never discussed having sex, but we've had it," I almost shouted. "And we also never discussed birth control, but you haven't really seemed to care much about that."

"Sally, I'm sorry." His lips thinned. "It was irresponsible of me, I know that, but I just wanted you so bad that I wasn't thinking."

"Yeah, I get it. The sex was too good. I was too good. You

173

felt too good." I rolled my eyes. "I get that sex means more to you than a relationship."

"What are you talking about? I told you that I liked you. This is about more than sex."

"Is it?" I said and gazed at him, my eyes piercing into his, looking for honest answers to my questions.

"What are you asking me, Sally?" He chewed on his lower lip and I could see his heart beating as his chest rose quickly.

"What do you think?" I cocked my head to the side, not even caring that I was putting my cards on the line.

"Are you saying you want to be in a relationship with me?" The words tripped out of his mouth uncomfortably. "Are you saying that you want to date me? That you want to be my girlfriend?" He continued to stare at me with an impassive face and I just stared back at him, having no idea what he was thinking. Did he think I was crazy? Was he scared out of his mind?

"I would like to think that the person I'm sleeping with would also want me to be his girlfriend," I said simply.

"We haven't even been on any dates," he said slowly, his eyes changing into an emotion akin to fear. "We don't even know if we'd be compatible in a relationship. We don't even know if we'd get on well."

"Okay." I nodded, his answer telling me everything we needed to know.

"Okay?" He frowned. "That's all you have to say?"

"What do you want me to say?" I said, and I could feel my entire body trembling. Tears were welling up in my eyes and I just stared at him. So handsome, so sexy, so lost. My love. My everything. My nothing, because he wasn't mine.

"I don't know," he said. "Maybe that you'll just go along with things how they are and then we can rethink everything later."

"Rethink what, Cody?" I shook my head at him. "What is there to rethink?"

"How we feel."

"I know how I feel, you know how you feel." I shrugged. "There's nothing to rethink."

"Sally, you're really confusing me. This is the first time we've ever had a conversation like this. I don't know what you feel. I don't know what you want." He shook his head.

"Then I'm just another crazy girl, I suppose." I was starting to get angry. "How can you not know how I feel, Cody? Are you an idiot? Are you blind? Do you think I would just come back with you and sleep with you because you're such a smooth talker?"

"Maybe." He cracked a grin, but it quickly fell from his face when he realized that I wasn't in the mood for jokes.

"Everything is a joke to you." I shook my head and reached down for my clothes. "I'm not going to do this anymore."

"Do what?" He looked baffled and I could almost laugh. He really seemed to have no idea that I was in love with him. "You're leaving? Did I do something wrong, Sally? I'm so confused right now."

"You're not the only one who's confused." I pulled on my clothes. "I'm bloody confused and angry."

"What?" He grabbed my arms and held me still. "Look at me, Sally. You need to tell me what's going on. I can't read your mind. What the hell happened when I went down to watch football? I truly don't understand."

"It doesn't matter. I'm over it. I'm over you." I was hurt and frustrated and all the hurt was coming out. I didn't even care that he didn't even know what I was talking about.

"Over me?" He frowned. "Sally?"

We both paused as my phone beeped from under the duvet. He pulled back from me and frowned. "Your phone's in the bed?" He walked over and pulled the duvet off and grabbed my phone. I bit down on my lower lip, hoping that it wasn't Luke texting me. *Please, please don't let it be Luke texting me again*, I thought. Please let it be Mila asking me how I'm doing. Or something like that. The silence as he grabbed the phone and looked at the screen was painful, but I knew as soon as the tension hit the air and his angry red face looked at me that I wasn't going to be so lucky. I knew before he even said anything that it was Luke who had texted me and that he had read the text.

"So you're still talking to Luke," he said, his voice deceptively low.

"Yeah, I am." I nodded slowly. "Well, he texted me today. To apologize and explain what happened the other day."

"Before or after we had sex?" He pursed his lips. "Before or after you went crazy?"

"I didn't go crazy." I glared at him. "And this has nothing to do with him." I waved my arms between us. "This has everything to do with us and just us."

"Yeah, okay." He shook his head in disgust. "Don't even try and lie to me, Sally. Just an hour ago you were screaming out my name and now you're putting on your clothes, mumbling some bullshit about relationships and being confused and not explaining shit to me. And you're telling me this has nothing to do with the text message you just got from some dipshit guy that you've been seeing the last week, who wanted to put ice cream on your body and lick it off."

"What the hell are you talking about?" I shook my head at him. "You're fucking crazy. I never said he wanted to put ice cream on my body and lick it off. *You* did."

"If you want that so bad, I have some vanilla downstairs. I can go and get it and lick it off you now. If that's what you want."

"You're a pig," I screamed at him, my eyes wide. I wasn't even sure how we had descended so low so quickly. "How dare you?"

"I'm all about sex, right? So I guess I dare a lot of things. Shit, why don't you bend over right now and I'll stick it in your ass as well?"

"Cody." I stared at him in shock, unable to believe he'd just said that. He looked back at me, his face looking as shocked as mine and he handed me my phone silently. "I think I'm going to leave now," I said softly as I grabbed my phone.

"Whatever." He turned around and walked out of the room, leaving me standing there with trembling fingers. I pressed down on the phone to see the text that Luke had sent me, that had sent everything over the edge, and sighed. *Also, I just wanted to say that our kiss the other night was magical. I think I saw a shooting star when we pulled apart and I wanted you to know that I made a wish. My wish was that every kiss we shared would be as special as that one. Hopefully it will still come true.*

I looked at the screen for another few seconds and tears streamed down my face and onto the phone as I read Luke's words. Why was this so complicated? Why wasn't it Cody who was sending me these sweet texts? And more importantly, how was it possible to feel like I liked two guys? And how did I get over these thoughts and feelings? Everything was a real mess and I knew I had no idea what to do to figure it out. Not that it really mattered. As far as I was concerned, I was done with Cody once and for all, and this time I meant it.

CHAPTER SEVENTEEN

Cody

I HEARD THE door slam behind Sally as she left my apartment, and I continued to sit on my couch for a few seconds, seething. I had no idea why she was so angry and I couldn't believe she was playing me. Did she really have feelings for Luke? Reading in that text message that they'd kissed had made me see red. She'd kissed him? I'd been texting her every day. I'd been thinking about her. Worrying she'd been mad at me. I'd been there, hoping to see her and hoping she'd been going through the same thing. And now I find out that she's out making out with other guys? Perverted guys who wanted to lick ice cream off of her. I was pissed. How dare she play me? I could feel myself growing angry. How dare she pretend she was angry because we'd had sex and try and make it seem like the reason she was angry was because I'd said I didn't think we were ready to be boyfriend and girlfriend.

What the hell did she expect?

Would any reasonable woman think they were dating some-one they'd never been on a date with before? She should have said she wanted to go on a date if that was what she wanted. How was I to know? I mean really, I'm not a mind-reader.

The more I thought about it, the more I realized she was just using me. She'd slept with me because she was on the rebound with Luke because she thought he'd dumped her and wasn't interested, and then he'd texted and she'd felt guilty and now was taking it out on me.

I was pissed.

She'd used me.

I sat on the couch, seething, angry at her, but in my heart I knew I wasn't completely right. I knew that inside there was more going on here and I just didn't want to acknowledge it. I shifted on the couch and grabbed my phone. There was only one person I could call right now. Only one person who would know what to say and how to help.

"Cody?" Mila's voice sounded surprised as she answered the phone.

"Yes, it's me, your stupid big brother," I said sheepishly into the phone.

"What's going on? Where's Sally? Isn't she with you? Oh, my God, is everything okay? Was there an accident?" Mila's voice sounded anxious.

"She's fine. I mean, at least she's not hurt, from an accident." I sighed. "I don't know what's going on. I need to talk to you. Like, really talk to you. I know you're Sally's best friend and you don't want to betray her confidence, but I need to talk to you, Mila. You're my sister and you're the only one I trust to be honest with me, and I really need your honesty right now."

"What's going on, Cody?" Mila's voice was worried. "Please tell me everything is okay."

"I don't know." I sighed down the phone line. "I really don't know."

"What happened?" Mila sighed. "Hold on, I'm going to go and sit down."

"Yeah, you should do that." I sighed again and closed my eyes. "I don't even know what's going on with Sally. I don't understand her, Mila. I don't understand what she wants or doesn't want."

"Start from the beginning," Mila said softly.

"I'm sure you know we've had sex. Don't lecture me, I know it was foolish of me," I said, even though I knew I would have done it again in a heartbeat.

"I'm not even going to comment," Mila said. "I'm assuming you guys copulated again this afternoon?"

"Don't make it sound so crude."

"I'm not making it sound anything," she said snidely. "Just continue."

"I thought we were on the same page. I apologized to her about hurting her feelings. Told her I thought she'd been ignoring me, but she told me she'd just been busy. I guess with that fool, Luke."

"He's not a fool. He's a nice guy."

"Uh huh, did you know they'd kissed?" I said angrily, feeling a spark of jealousy running through my stomach again, and I clenched my fists.

"Yes," she said simply. "How do you know?"

"I saw his text."

"He texted her?" She sounded surprised. "What did he say?"

"How am I supposed to know? All I saw was a text saying how all he could think about was their passionate kiss," I said bitterly.

"Wow, he said that?"

"Mila!" I almost shouted. "He didn't use those exact words. I can't remember what he said, exactly. Who the fuck cares? This is about me, not about this schmuck. Whose brother are you?"

"I'm no one's brother?" She laughed.

"Ugh, you know what I mean. Whose sister are you?"

"You know I always have your back, Cody," she said softly.

"I take it you're upset that Sally kissed Luke. Is this what this call is about? Did you guys argue about the kiss? And how did you see the text message on her phone? Were you creeping through her texts?"

"I would never snoop through someone's phone," I said with a sigh. "She was getting upset with me and acting all irrationally and shouting at me and her phone beeped, so I very kindly went to get it for her and I found it stuffed under the sheets and saw his name and text on her phone. She'd been texting with him in the bed that we'd just made love in."

"Really?" Mila's voice was dubious. "That doesn't sound like Sally."

"Well, maybe you don't really know Sally. Maybe *I* don't really know Sally. Who knew she was a player?"

"Sally isn't a player," Mila said. "You know that."

"How am I supposed to know that?" I said. "She's in my bed texting another guy."

"Okay, Cody, what help do you want from me?" Mila sighed in frustration. "I'm not sure exactly what you called me for, since you don't seem to want to listen to what I have to say."

"I want to know what Sally's problem is. What game is she playing with me? I want to know what I'm supposed to do now. Am I supposed to text her? Call her? Am I supposed to just let her go on with Luke? Ignore her? Go back to being friends and pretend everything is okay?"

"What do you want to do?"

"I don't know," I snapped. "I don't know. I don't know what game she's playing with me. I don't know what she wants from me."

"What do you want, Cody?"

"I don't know." My heart started thudding. "I want to be with her. I want to spend time with her. I want to kiss her. I want to hold her hand. I want to talk to her. I want to be her shoulder to lean on. I want her to come to me when she's sad. I just, I don't know..." My voice trailed off. "What's happening to me, Mila?"

"You have to figure it out yourself, Cody," Mila said softly. "I think you'll get there, but you need to figure it out yourself."

"I need to talk to Sally." I sighed. "I just don't even know why she was so upset."

"Do you really not know?" Mila cleared her throat. "You're my brother and I love you, but you cannot be this dense. I know you can't be this dense."

"What do you mean?"

"You knew Sally had a crush on you when we were younger," Mila suddenly snapped. "I know that you knew, because TJ and I have talked about it before."

"Yeah, so?"

"So have you never considered the possibility that her crush never really faded? Be honest now, bro. Come on, now."

"I don't know," I said softly, not sure how to answer. "Maybe? I don't know. I've never really thought it."

"You're selfish, Cody. You're really, really selfish." Mila sounded pissed. "You know in your heart of hearts why Sally is upset. You know what's going on, but you don't want to acknowledge it. You don't want to be any more uncomfortable than you have to be. You think you can just sleep with girls and lead them on and just do what you want without any emotional entanglements? You think people don't have feelings? You think you can pull and tug at her heartstrings and not have any repercussions? You think you can become close to someone and just be in some weird friend-zone where you fuck forever? That's all you're comfortable with. And God knows why you're so scared of relationships. I don't get it. I don't get you. You can't play people like this, Cody. You can't pretend ignorance. You can't call the girl crazy. You can't make it seem like you're an innocent bystander in all of this. It's not fair and it's not right. You need to grow up. You need to look a little deeper. You need to stop being so bloody selfish and think about how others might be thinking and what your actions and words might be doing. Think about someone else's feelings for once and act based upon that. Stop acting and doing things because you're a jealous little boy who doesn't want to share his toys."

"Anything else?" I said, processing in shock what she'd said to me.

"Yeah, figure it out soon," she snapped. "Get it together, Cody, please just get it together." And then I heard the phone slamming down.

I dropped my phone onto my couch and sat back and tried to think about everything she had just said to me. She'd been harsh, but maybe she'd also been partially right? Was I being selfish? And if I was, what did that mean? Where did I go from here? What did I want? What did Sally want? And would I ever be able to figure it out?

THREE DAYS—THAT was how long it took me to call her. I thought maybe she'd call me or text me to apologize, but of course she didn't. I wasn't even really sure why I thought she would. It wasn't like she seemed to even care about me anymore. I missed the days when she would text me randomly throughout the day. I'd grown so accustomed to her random texts that I hadn't realized how much they meant to me, until now. And now that they'd stopped, I would have given anything to just get one. At least then I would know she was thinking about me. If even for just a few seconds. She crossed my mind every moment of the day and I had no idea if she even thought of me at all.

The first time I called, it rang three times and went to voicemail. I wasn't sure if that meant it had just gone to voicemail by itself or if she had sent me to voicemail. I was hoping it was the former, so I ended up calling her a second time just a few minutes later. Maybe her phone hadn't rung or maybe it had been off. Maybe she'd even been trying to call me at the same time. This time the phone rang two times and went to voicemail, and I frowned. Either her phone wasn't working properly or she was sending me to voicemail. I'd call her one last time and then I'd leave a voicemail. The third time I called, it didn't even ring once. It went straight to voicemail. I gripped the phone and hung up angrily. Had she turned her phone off or was her phone broken? I knew it was highly unlikely that her phone was broken, but I wasn't sure why she would turn her phone off. Were my calls really that annoying? I looked down at the phone and called her again a fourth time. Once again, it went straight to voicemail. I hung up. And called again. Voicemail. I dropped the phone on the couch, walked to the kitchen, grabbed some water and took a few deep breaths and walked back to my phone. I grabbed my phone, looked at the screen to see if I had any missed calls or missed text messages, and sighed when I saw none. I pressed redial on her number and frowned as it went straight to voicemail again.

"Sally, it's me—Cody. Call me back. We need to talk," I said and then hung up. I groaned as I hung up. My voice had sounded accusatory and my message had been too short. If she listened to this message she was unlikely to call me back. So I decided to call her back and leave one more message. It might make me look like a psycho, but it was better than looking like a jerk. I called back one more time and this time the phone rang. My heart stilled as I waited to see if she was going to pick up the phone. My heart fell pretty quickly as it went to voicemail again. I cleared my throat and started to leave my new message.

"Hi, Sally, it's me—Cody. I hope you're doing well. I'm sorry about the other day. I'm sorry we got so angry at each other. I'd really like to talk to you to see if we can figure this out. Please call me back. I'd love to see you as soon as possible. I miss you." I pressed the pound sign this time instead of hanging up so that I could re-listen to the message to see how it sounded and if I wanted to change it before submitting it to her ears. I figured I sounded like a bit of a pussy, but sincere enough, so I left it and accepted the message. All I had to do was wait now. Wait for her to call me back. Wait for her to tell me she was willing to see me. Wait for her to tell me exactly what she wanted. I sat back on the couch and closed my eyes, hoping I didn't have to wait too long.

CHAPTER EIGHTEEN

Sally

THERE'S A FEELING at the end, when you know it's the end. It's a feeling of despair, of hurt, of knowing there's nothing you can do to change your fate. It's the feeling of knowing you will never be enough. Knowing that no part of you will ever be enough, and it's heartbreaking. It makes you wonder, "What's wrong with me? Why am I not lovable? Why am I not enough?" It's the moment that makes you want to not be alive. It's the moment when you give up all hope. It's the moment you know you will never be pretty enough, smart enough, happy enough, rich enough. It's the moment when you doubt everything you ever believed. Sometimes I wonder how I got to such a low spot. It's the moment I wondered, *Why me?* It's the moment I just wanted to fade into oblivion. We grow up believing that one day our fairytale will come true, but what if that's never the case? What if we're destined to be alone? What if we're not lovable? What if there's something wrong with us? Even though we try to be the best person we can be, what if above everything else, we are just never destined to find love or have happiness? Life should mean more than having a partner. It should mean more than loving and being loved. But what if that's all you ever wanted? What if all you ever wanted was for someone to look at you with adoration in their eyes? What if all you ever wanted was to feel that someone understood you? Cared about you? Loved you? What if all you ever wanted was to be enough?

It's hard feeling like you're not enough. It's hard feeling there's something lacking in you. Knowing there's something you will never, ever have. Something that you see everyone else has but you. I just don't understand. Why not me? I don't understand what's wrong with me. What can I change? What can I do? What can I feel? What can I say? Can I be skinnier? How can I be prettier? How can I be more desirable? How can I get smarter? What can I do? If only I knew.

If only I knew.

If I only knew why Cody didn't love me. If only I knew why he didn't care. Why he didn't understand. Why he didn't want to be with me. But I didn't. I couldn't understand why I could love him so much and he could be so oblivious. I could spend my life trying to figure it out, and yet I would never understand. There's a voice in my head that screams and shouts at me. A voice that wonders why I can't just let it go. It's a voice that hates me being me. It hates me feeling like this. Sometimes I wonder if I have a split personality. Sometimes I wonder if I have serious mental issues. Any sane person, any normal person, would have moved on by now. They would have gotten the memo. I got the memo, several times, and ripped it to pieces. I deserve the heartache I feel. I deserve not feeling good enough. I deserve it for constantly putting myself in this position. And though I deserve it, that doesn't stop me from shedding tears for myself. It doesn't stop it from hurting. If only I could figure out a way to stop the hurt and pain.

"I CAN'T BREATHE," I whispered over the phone to Mila as soon as she answered. I was sobbing, but trying to mask my voice, so I was talking as low as possible.

"What?" she said loudly. "Are you sick?"

"No…maybe. I don't know." Tears were streaming down my face and I took a deep breath. "I just can't breathe."

"What's going on, Sally?" Mila sounded worried, but I could hear her yawning.

"Sorry for waking you up," I said, feeling guilty. "Cody left me some messages. I just don't know what to do anymore."

"You can wake me up at any time. You know that." Her voice was loud again and I could hear TJ in the background mumbling something. "It's Sally," she whispered, and I smiled as I heard her saying something to him, telling him to go back to sleep. "Hold on, Sally."

"Okay," I said and lay back in the bed and closed my eyes. My heart felt heavy and I clutched the phone next to my ear as I pulled the covers up over my head. The room felt like it was spinning and I felt like I just wanted to never wake up again. I knew I shouldn't feel so morbid, that my situation wasn't the end of the world, but I just couldn't stop feeling sorry for myself.

"I'm back," she said, her voice softer now. "What's going on?"

"I can't stop thinking about Cody," I said, my voice sounding foreign to my own ears.

"Did something happen?" Mila sounded worried. "Did he say something stupid?"

"No, yes, no." I sighed. "He left me a voicemail."

"Hurtful?"

"No, it was really nice. It wasn't anything, but it meant everything to me. He sounded really sincere." My voice cracked.

"Oh? Is that a bad thing?"

"He's always on my mind, Mila. When I heard his voicemail, I felt so happy. I felt on top of the world. I literally went from feeling despondent and down, to flying. It's not right that he should control my emotions this way. I'm just a nut-job." I groaned. "Why does he make me feel this way?"

"Because you love him," she said softly, and I groaned. "I'm sorry," she continued. "I know how hard this is for you."

"How can I stop loving him? I need to stop loving him. This is too hard. I don't want to deal with this anymore, Mila. I can't keep loving him. I don't know what to do. I don't even want to call him back. What's the point? Nothing ever changes. I'm always just chasing butterflies into the sky."

"I don't know," she said softly. "I'm so sorry."

"I think I need to cut him out of my life," I said, as much to myself as to her. "I need to just forget him completely."

"How are you going to do that?" she said, her words coming slowly. "He's my brother."

"I know," I said and I could feel my heart racing again. Only this time, it was with anxiety. "I don't know what else to do. This isn't healthy for me."

"So what about events that I invite you both to?"

"I won't be able to go. I'm sorry, Mila, but I need to do this for me. You just don't understand. I love him so much and I just can't seem to give him up and I just can't do this anymore."

"Is this because of Luke?"

"Luke?" I sighed. "I don't know. But, no, not really. Yes, I like Luke. I think he's handsome and really fun and for some reason he really likes me. And that makes me feel good. It makes me feel like I can be loved, but I also know that this isn't our time. I can't give him all of me and that's not fair to him. I can't do that to him just so I can get over Cody. It wouldn't be fair."

"Have you spoken to him?"

"No, I'm going to have lunch with him tomorrow. He deserves to know what's going on and I want to be as honest with him as I can. Maybe in the future we can see if we have a chance, but right now I need to focus on me and healing my heart. I need to focus on my life and being emotionally healthy. I need to purge Cody from my system. I'm done with this."

"So you've given up?" Mila's voice sounded sadder than I'd ever heard it before, her tone showcasing the hurt in my heart.

"If you want to call it that." I sighed, not wanting her to make me feel worse about my decision.

"You don't love Cody anymore?"

"I don't know what I feel for him anymore. I mean, yes, I love him. I'll always love him, but I don't want to be in love with him. I want to completely forget him. I want to forget I ever met him. I want to rid him from my mind completely." I shook my head, though that wasn't completely honest. In my heart of hearts, I knew.

"Being around Luke has really made me realize how much Cody just isn't into me. Luke is a good guy," I said, my voice suddenly getting loud. "He's a really good guy. And I like him and he likes me. And he makes me laugh. And he thinks I'm pretty. And he likes being with me. And he asks me on dates. And he texts me. And..." My voice trailed off as I heard Mila breathing into the phone. "I need someone who wants me, Mila. I need someone who can love me. And I've thought about it. I've wondered if I'm being bad to Luke by dating him, knowing I still have feelings for Cody, and that's why I'm ending it with him. And I really like Luke. When I'm with him, I don't think of Cody. Well, not really. Only sometimes. And most of the time I'm okay. Sometimes I even think I could fall for Luke. Sometimes I even think I could love him. Not like I love Cody, at least that's how I feel now. And do you know how that makes me feel? It makes me feel like I'm never going to find love. You ask me if I still love Cody like it's that easy. Like that makes my decision easier. The problem is, I love Cody so much. The problem is that he's my entire world and I'm nothing to him."

"We won't be sisters," Mila said softly.

"We were never going to be sisters." I sighed, tears wanting to well up in my eyes. "Cody doesn't care for me like that. I don't know what his game is. I don't know why he acts jealous and pretends like he cares but then never does anything. I don't know and I don't care anymore. My heart can't take it anymore. I've lost a piece of myself, Mila. I can't explain it, but a piece of my soul has died. A piece of me is forever gone and the more I hope, the more I love, the more I wait, the more I feel myself fading into oblivion, not caring, not dreaming, not wondering, not living."

"You should talk to Cody. Call him back and see what he has to say."

"And tell him what?" I sighed. "It's not his problem. You can't blame someone for not loving you. I don't need to have another conversation with him. I'm sure he feels bad. I'm sure he wishes that he could love me. I know he cares about me. I know he wants me in his life, but I want more than sex. I want more than a good friend. I want a man who would die for me. I want a man who feels my pain. I want a man who can feel my heart. I want a man who loves me so much that he can't go a day without seeing or talking to me. I want a man who adores me so much that he thinks the sun rises and sets with me. I want a man who thinks about me first thing in the morning and last thing at night. I want a man who would take my last breath for me. I don't want a man who makes me feel like I can't breathe. I feel like I'm the walking dead, Mila. I feel like I can't even go on another day like this."

"I wish I could slap him," Mila mumbled and I could hear tears falling from her eyes.

"Why are you crying?" I asked her softly, feeling myself wanting to cry as well.

"Because you're in so much pain and I can feel it." She sobbed and I could hear the tears running faster now. "I don't want to lose you, Sally. And I don't want you to lose yourself, either. I feel like my brother has changed you, torn you down, and now you're trembling like a flower in a brisk wind."

"Oh, Mila." I grabbed my phone tightly. "I don't even know what to say."

"You don't have to be strong now, Sally." Mila's voice became strong. "You can cry. You can cry and sob and hug me tight any day of the week. I'm here for you. I love you. You're my best friend. You're my soul mate. I will always be here for you."

"Oh, Mila." I started crying. "I wish you were here right now. You don't even know how I feel right now." My tears started falling like raindrops in a thunderstorm, heavy and dark, and I could feel my nose running as well. I could hear Mila crying, and then I started crying even harder. It was like I could finally let it all out. All the pain and hurt and confusion. All the dreams and hopes. I was letting them all go. And perhaps that was the hardest thing of all.

It had been easier when there was hope that things would change. It had hurt, but I had always imagined there was a beckoning light at the end of the tunnel.

But now...now there was nothing. Giving up all hope and letting go of Cody was the end. It was the end of every childish dream I'd ever had about the two of us. It was the end of my one-true-love fantasy. It was the end of my lifelong quest to end up with my soul mate. Cody and I were never going to be. We were never going to get married and sing songs to our children. He was never going to wake me up in the morning, gazing adoringly in my eyes and whispering he loved me. We were never going to grow old together and tell each other stories. We were never going to anything. There was never going to be a 'we'. That killed me. Knowing that made me die a million deaths, but inside I could also feel a little flower blooming. A flower that was ready to bloom under another sun. A flower that was ready for some happiness and no more pain. A flower that was ready for the dawn of a new day.

"WHY WON'T YOU talk to me, Sally?" Cody stood on my doorstep, and I felt like I wanted to pass out. "What's going on?"

"Nothing." I shook my head. "What are you doing here?"

"You're not answering my calls. My emails. I sent you some messages on Facebook. I texted you." His eyes searched mine. "You haven't responded to anything."

"What do you care?" I said bitterly. "It's not like you always respond. I just didn't get around to it yet."

"You always respond," he said, his face unsure and red. "You don't ignore me."

"What do you want, Cody?" I stood at the door, just waiting for him to leave. I didn't want to talk to him. Just seeing him was breaking my heart. I didn't want to deal with this.

"Can I come in?"

"Why?" I took a deep breath. "I just don't have much time right now."

"I thought we were friends," he said softly.

"Yeah, we are." I nodded.

"Once, you called me your best friend," he said with a small smile. "Remember?"

"We all say things we don't mean." I shrugged.

"You're one of my best friends," he said softly. "You know

that, right?"

I didn't respond. I didn't know what to say. What did it even matter anymore? What did anything matter? I felt too numb inside. Too heartbroken. Too empty. *I hate you* was all I could think as I stared at him. I hate you for making me feel this way. I hate you for making me have so much self-doubt. I hate you for me not being able to let go. I hate you for not letting go of me when you knew you didn't love me. I hate you. I hate you. I hate you.

"So how have you been?" he asked me, his face somber as we stood there in awkward silence.

"Good, you?" I gave him a half-hearted smile, not wanting him to know how uncomfortable I felt inside. Not wanting him to know he had made me lose a part of myself and that I'd been awful while trying to pretend, even to myself, that I was doing well.

"Not great," he said, his face looking sad. "But better now that I'm getting to see you."

"Okay." I nodded. "So what did you want to talk about?"

"Everything." He shrugged. "I just want to feel better about this situation."

"I'm not here to make you feel better about yourself, Cody. I'm sorry, but I've done that too much already. The only times you've really come to me haven't been about me. They've been because you were feeling down and out, and you needed me to make you feel better about yourself."

"That's not true." He looked at me with a hurt expression. "I care a lot about you."

"Yeah, yeah, I know that. You care oh so much about me." I rolled my eyes. "I get it, Cody. Look, I know we're friends, but I also know that I can't do this anymore."

"Do what?" His voice rose. "Do we have to get into an argument already? I really hoped we could just talk everything out."

"Sure, let's talk it out," I said with a sigh. What really was there left to talk about?

"What should we talk about?" he asked, looking at me with an alert expression that made me want to scream and shout.

"Cody, you called me. You wanted to meet up with me, so if you want to talk, you need to start the conversation." I was not going to make this easy for him. I was over it. Really and truly over it.

"I'm trying to. Can you stop being so difficult, please?"

"I'm not being difficult." I groaned, not sure if I was going to be able to do this with him.

"Okay," he said simply as he pursed his lips. "If you say so."

"I do say so," I said, not able to stop a small smile from crossing my face. He looked back at me and smiled back as well. I felt my heart skipping a beat as we both smiled at each other. For a second everything was all right in the world again.

"I miss you," he started again and gave me another small smile. "I miss talking to you. I miss getting your texts. I miss you telling me off for not texting. I miss you dreaming of me. I miss you telling me about your dreams. I miss you wanting to hang out. I miss your random messages. I miss you being there in small ways."

"I annoyed you," I said, not wanting to think anything positive. Not wanting to believe that he really missed me in any way important.

"That's what I said. How I acted." He sighed, his eyes bleak. "I know that. I know I hurt you. I know I made you think I didn't care. I know I haven't been the friend you needed. I'm so sorry for so many things."

"It's fine. I forgive you."

"Please, can I come in?" He pursed his lips. "Can we have this conversation in your living room as opposed to at your front door?"

"Fine." I sighed then, and opened the door wider. "Come in."

"Thanks." He stepped into the doorway and paused as I closed the door. "You look really pretty today."

"Thanks," I said, not looking at him. I didn't want to look into his eyes. I didn't want to see his handsome face. I didn't want my heart to skip the beats it always did when he was around. I didn't want to be so affected by him, every damn time I saw him.

"So have you missed me?" he asked softly, and I could feel him stepping closer to me. I froze as I felt his fingers on my chin, lifting my face to stare at him, his eyes hopeful.

"I don't know what you want me to say," I mumbled, a piece of me dying inside. And another part of me feeling the heat of fire, and hope that had never fully extinguished. That I knew now would never be extinguished, no matter how much I willed it away. He was always going to come back. He was always going to keep kindling it. And this feeling—this love—it was never going to leave me. I was doomed to love him forever. I just needed to learn how to live with it and not let it ruin my life.

CHAPTER NINETEEN

Cody

SALLY STOOD IN front of me, her face tired and her eyes red and every little inch of me felt like a piece of crap. I'd come over here wanting to accuse her of being in love with Luke. Wanting to tell her that she'd ditched me for him. Wanting to play the innocent victim because I was hurt that she hadn't returned my calls and texts. I was an asshole, I realized that now. And more importantly, Mila had been right. I was selfish. I was really selfish. I was seeing this all through my own eyes. I was feeling my own hurt. I was dealing with my own pain. And I wasn't seeing it through the perspective of Sally. I felt like grabbing a dagger and sticking it through my own heart for being such a selfish, asinine idiot.

"I lied," I said as I stepped back from her and pursed my lips. I let out a huge sigh and ran my hands through my hair. I could tell from the expression on her face that she had no idea what was going on.

"You lied about what?" she said, her eyes barely able to look into mine.

"I lied when I pretended I didn't know what you were talking about the other day. When you talked about relationships." I pursed my lips.

"Oh," she said and looked down. "It's fine. It doesn't matter.

I shouldn't have brought it up. It wasn't really relevant to us."

"Of course it was relevant." I sighed again as I listened to her. What had happened to her spunk? Had I done this to her? Had I made her this shell of a person? "I'm an idiot, Sally. A fucking idiot. You can hit me, beat me, spank me, do whatever you want to me. I deserve it."

"What are you talking about?" She looked up at me in confusion, blinking slowly. I wanted to reach out and pull her into my arms. I wanted to kiss away her pain. I wanted to tell her I was sorry for being such a jackass. I wanted to go back in time and redo so many things, but I knew that none of that was possible. At least not know.

"I'm not a complicated guy, you know," I started mumbling. "I like beer. I like sports. I like women." I sighed. "I had a good childhood, have good friends. Everything has been pretty easy for me. I like my life. I like it being uncomplicated. I don't do complicated. I don't do entanglements. I've never had to worry about someone depending on me, needing me. I've never had to worry about my own feelings becoming tied to someone else, either. I've never had that happen to me before."

"What?" she said softly.

"I've never felt bad because I thought someone was upset at me before." I gave her a look. "I guess I'm emotionally immature, but I've never cared that much about a person that my own feelings have changed based on how they're feeling."

"I see," she said, but her expression showed that she wasn't really following what I was saying.

"I've never experienced jealousy before, either. I never knew what it felt like to lie awake all night, wondering what someone was doing, where they were, who they were talking to, if they were thinking of me. I've never known that I could be jealous of my own sister."

"You've been jealous of Mila?"

I nodded and then grabbed her hand. "Can we go and sit down? Please?"

"Okay." She nodded and we walked towards her living room and sat down on the couch. I looked over at her and I could feel my heart strings tightening. How had I not known how I felt about Sally before all of this? How had I ignored the feeling in my heart? Had I been that dumb and blind?

"I was jealous of the fact that Mila got to talk to you, to spend time with you. I was jealous that she was the one you were going to. I wanted it to be me. I wanted to hear from you. I wanted to be your one."

"I could hardly go to you about you," Sally said softly. "Anyways, what do you care?"

"Oh, Sally, I've really and truly confused you, haven't I? I suppose it makes sense, though. I've been so confused myself. Not only was I lying to you, but I was lying to myself as well."

"Lying about what, exactly?"

"Lying that I didn't care. Lying that I didn't know that you cared. Lying that I thought this was casual. Lying that I was okay with it being casual. Lying that I was okay with you going on dates. Lying that I was okay with you dating Luke. Lying that I wanted to go on dates with other women. Lying that I was thinking about other women aside from you. Lying that I wasn't thinking about you all the time. Lying that we were just friends. Lying that I didn't want more. Lying that I couldn't give you more. Lying that this wasn't something special. Lying that the feeling in my heart wasn't love." I paused then and watched her face as she gasped and stared at me with wide eyes. I knew in that instant that whatever she'd felt for me hadn't faded completely.

The light that shone in her eyes, the way she looked at me,

the sudden glow that she had... It meant something. It meant I still had a chance. All I needed was one last chance. All I needed was for Sally to know that I knew I'd screwed up. I knew that I had broken her, not intentionally, never intentionally. It killed me to think she'd been in pain because I'd been such an idiot, but I wanted to make it up to her. I needed to make it up to her. I needed her to know I wanted to spend the rest of my life making it up to her, showing her that I wasn't going to be afraid of my feelings anymore. I wanted to step out of my comfort zone. I wanted to give her everything she wanted. I wanted to stop lying to her and myself. I wanted to be the man she wanted me to be. I wanted to be the man she thought I was. I wanted to prove to her that my love and my heart were hers forever and I never wanted her to ever have to doubt that again.

CHAPTER TWENTY

Sally

I THOUGHT MY heart was going to pop out of my chest. That's how fast it was racing. I felt like I was in the *Twilight Zone* and I wanted to pinch myself. Was I really and truly here with Cody and had he really just said that he loved me? This couldn't be happening. This was all too surreal. Cody was not here, with me, in my living room, telling me he'd been lying to me. Things like this didn't happen in real life. People didn't all of a sudden love you. He didn't all of a sudden love me. Prayers didn't really come true. I didn't understand. *I must be dreaming. I must be dreaming.* I pinched myself and it hurt and I knew then that this wasn't a dream. My heart started racing then and I could feel life stirring back into my cold body. Was Cody really here making me a believer once again?

"I'm glad I met you as a little girl," Cody said with a small smile on his face, and I frowned.

"Why?" I gazed into his eyes that were staring at me openly with love, and I swallowed hard.

"Because."

"Because why?" I wanted to ask him if this was some sort of cruel joke, but I was scared of his answer.

"Because this way I know I'm your true love."

"Cody! Is this a joke?" I looked at him in shock. Was that

something romantic coming out of his mouth? And what did he know about true love? And did he think I loved him? Oh, God, did he know?

"Of course not." He shook his head.

"How do you know you're my true love, then?" I grinned at him, unable to stop myself. I didn't care if he knew I loved him, if he loved me as well.

"Because you're mine," he said simply, and my heart froze.

"Say that again," I whispered.

"Say what?" He grimaced, looking slightly embarrassed, and I laughed at the expression on his face. So awkward and slightly worried. Maybe he wasn't as sure about my feelings as he was letting on.

"You know."

"I know nothing."

"Cody!"

"That's my name."

"I'm your true love?"

"I said it."

"You don't believe in true love, though, as you've told me several times."

"I believe in you," he said simply, his eyes shining brightly, and I felt like the sun had come out in my living room, such was the light shining through my heart and soul.

"Thank you." I grabbed his hand and squeezed it tightly and I felt his fingers grasping mine. I looked over at his face and he had a small smile on his face.

"Don't go expecting me to send any sappy poetry or lines from books, though." He laughed.

"You'd love it." I grinned, though. I knew I would love it as well.

"Ugh, never."

"What is life without love?" I asked him softly, giddy with happiness.

"Life," he said, and I looked over at him and glared. "What?" he said with a bigger smile. "Life without love is still life."

"Sometimes, I can't believe we're soul mates." I shook my head. "You're so cynical."

"So you think we're soul mates?" He started grinning at me, and I rolled my eyes at him.

"I think that's been obvious." I laughed. "I haven't really hidden it that well, have I?" I gazed at him tenderly, hardly believing this moment was happening.

"Say it," he said, looking into my eyes deeply.

"Say what?" I teased him.

"You know," he said, his eyes beguiling, begging me to put him out of his misery. "Say it," he said again, almost begging.

"Say what?" I said again, teasing him, needing him to know it meant a lot to me. As much as it meant to him.

"Say you love me," he said, gripping my hands as he waited.

"I love you, Cody Brookstone," I said sweetly and simply, kissing his lips softly. "I love you with all my heart. I always have and I always will."

16448257R00125

Printed in Great Britain
by Amazon